# THE NAME ON THE BULLET

**Totally gripping detective fiction**

## JOHN DEAN

Paperback published by The Book Folks

London, 2023



This book is a work of fiction. Names, characters, businesses, organizations, places and events are either the product of the author's imagination or are used fictitiously. Any resemblance to actual persons, living or dead, events or locales is entirely coincidental.



ISBN 978-1-80462-073-1

www.thebookfolks.com

*The Name on the Bullet is the eleventh standalone title in a series of British detective mysteries featuring Detective Chief Inspector John Blizzard. Information about the other novels and a list of characters can be found at the back of this book.*

# Chapter one

The first glimmer of daylight was beginning to streak the sky above the northern city of Hafton as the police vehicles rolled along the quiet suburban road. The convoy, comprising a van, a minibus and an unmarked car, travelled slowly past the neatly kept semi-detached houses that stood in darkness along Rivermead Avenue, their occupants asleep and oblivious to what was about to happen. The vehicles came to a halt halfway down the road, where the minibus disgorged its cargo of officers, most of whom wore protective helmets and body armour. A tall, lean, clean-cut, short-haired man in plainclothes alighted from the passenger seat of the lead minibus and pointed to a semi-detached house.

'Number twenty-four,' he said in a low voice. 'The one with the green door. Whenever you're ready.'

'Seems a pity to ruin their sleep,' said one of the officers. He gave a broad grin. 'Still, mustn't grumble. God, I love my job!'

Detective Sergeant Alan Steele gave a slight smile.

'Go on then, play nice,' he said. The sergeant glanced at the cameraman who was standing nearby. 'They're going in now. You ready?'

Bob Harrold nodded, shouldered his camera and followed the police team as it moved quickly into position with an efficiency built up over many such raids. Within seconds, following a shouted warning, one of the officers had used the hydraulic ram to smash through the front door and, amid a splintering of timber and more hollered warnings, his colleagues barged their way into the property. Within a few moments, the officers had thundered up the stairs and dragged two bewildered-looking young men from their beds, taking them downstairs and outside to the waiting van. The whole operation had been carried out so rapidly that the vehicle's rear doors had been slammed shut by the time lights in nearby houses started to be switched on, curtains began to twitch, and the people of Rivermead Avenue realised what had happened.

Back inside number twenty-four, the plainclothes officer moved from room to room, watching in satisfaction at the growing number of finds which officers were bringing down to be placed on the kitchen table. Eventually, with the search at an end, the table was piled high with plastic bags containing pills and bundles of banknotes.

'An excellent haul,' said Steele. 'The best yet.'

He glanced at the cameraman. 'Do you want me to do a piece to camera?'

'Yeah, go on.'

'Do I look OK?' asked Steele. He ran a hand through his wavy brown hair.

'You'll do,' said the cameraman.

Steele gave his hair a final pat, checked that his tie was properly done up then gave himself a few moments to compose himself, stared into the camera and started talking with a fluency and confidence that came with more than a year of featuring in similar events.

'There must be the thick end of a thousand tablets here,' he said, gesturing to the table. 'And thanks to this morning's operation, they won't be going anyway near the city's young people. It just goes to show the importance of initiatives like Operation Javelin. Residents of areas like

Rivermead Avenue should not have their lives blighted by drug dealers and operations like the one this morning just go to show that if people give us information about drug dealers, we will act.'

He looked at the cameraman.

'OK?' he said.

'As ever,' said the cameraman.

* * *

A week later, Detective Superintendent Arthur Ronald listened to the sergeant's words to camera, gave an approving nod, picked the television remote control up off his desk and tapped the pause button, reducing Alan Steele to a shimmering image. The superintendent looked across the desk at Detective Chief Inspector John Blizzard.

'You have to admit it, John,' he said, 'we come out of this looking pretty good – despite your misgivings.'

It was just before 6pm and the two men were sitting in the superintendent's office at Abbey Road Police Station, sipping from mugs of tea as they watched the advance cut of the opening episode of the new series of the reality show *Arrested! Community Fightback*, which was due to be screened the following week.

'What's more, the chief will be delighted,' added Ronald. 'It's all on-message.'

'On-message!' snorted Blizzard. He had always struggled with force jargon. 'Only if the message you want to convey is corny.'

'Maybe it *is* corny,' said Ronald. 'But it's what the public wants to hear. The police working with the community to lock up drug dealers.'

'Yes, well, we can lock dealers up without someone sticking a camera in our faces every minute of the day,' said Blizzard with a scowl. 'There are no boundaries.'

Ronald gave a mock sigh of exasperation – he'd heard it all too many times from the inspector to take much notice. He released the pause button and the scene switched to images of the van delivering the prisoners to the collection of portable buildings that comprised Abbey Road Police Station, where Ronald was in charge of CID in the force's southern half and Blizzard ran the divisional department. They were very different men; the superintendent, a balding, smartly dressed man with ruddy cheeks and eyes with bags which sagged darkly, was the smooth-talking diplomat whereas Blizzard, with his tie at its customary half-mast, and his hair tousled, was the more outspoken of the two.

Back on the television screen, the pictures of the police station had been replaced by a caption, which read:

> *Following the raid, Carl Latheran and Edward Janes, both aged nineteen, were charged with numerous drugs-related offences. They admitted all the offences and are awaiting sentencing at Hafton Crown Court. Since Operation Javelin began thirteen months ago, twenty-four Hafton drug dealers have been sent to prison for terms ranging from six months to five years. Drugs with a street value of £1.2 million have been seized, along with £845,000 in cash and a selection of weapons, including knives and machetes.*

Alan Steele appeared on the screen again, this time standing in the custody suite as the protesting prisoners were brought in. The sergeant turned to face the camera.

'Operations like this serve as a reminder to the city's drug dealers that the phrase "community fightback" is not some sort of gimmick,' he said as the prisoners were led past him. 'Rather it is very much a reality. The men we have arrested can ponder on that thought as they sit in their prison cells.'

'Very smooth,' said Ronald with an approving nod.

Now, Steele was being filmed watching as the arrested men were booked in. One of them caught sight of the detective sergeant and uttered a series of profane threats, which were bleeped out.

'Doesn't it concern you when you receive threats like that?' asked the cameraman off-camera as the prisoner was taken to the cells by uniformed officers, still struggling and shouting his threats.

'It comes with the territory,' said Steele. 'It shows that we're doing our job properly. I'd be worried if the drug dealers weren't unhappy.'

'How important are the arrests this morning?' the cameraman asked.

'The arrest of every drug dealer is important, of course,' said Steele. 'However, these two are particularly so. We've had reports of defective ecstasy tablets being sold in Hafton's nightclubs over recent weeks and several people have ended up in hospital, as a result. One sixteen-year-old was kept in for five days. We could well have saved lives by our actions today. That's worth having to listen to the odd empty threat, I would suggest.'

'He really is very good,' said Ronald as the credits started to roll.

There was a knock on the door and Alan Steele entered the office.

'Ah, the man of the hour,' said Ronald. He gestured for the sergeant to take a seat. 'We've just been looking at the new series.'

'What do you think?' asked Steele.

'It's excellent,' said Ronald. 'You'll need an agent if this carries on.'

'Actually, that why I'm here.' Steele hesitated. 'See, the television company has offered me the chance to do some more work with them.'

'What kind of work?' asked Blizzard suspiciously.

'They want me to be one of the presenters on a new show that they're pitching to the networks,' said Steele. 'It's a bit like *Crimewatch* but with celebrities doing the presenting. They want me to front it with Gemma Carlisle.'

'And who is Gemma Carlisle when she's at home?' asked Blizzard.

'The woman who interviewed me for *The One Show* last year. They reckon there was a bit of on-screen chemistry between us.'

'I've never heard of her,' said Blizzard.

'You must have,' said Steele. 'She presents *Celebrity Vet School.* Who can forget her and Christopher Biggins delivering the lamb?'

Blizzard still looked blank.

'Well, whoever she is,' he said, 'I hope that you turned them down. You've got enough to do here. You're a police officer, remember.'

'Yes, well, that's the thing,' said Steele. He looked uneasily at Blizzard. 'I'd have to leave the job.'

Blizzard stared at him.

'Leave?' he said.

'They say that there'd be other projects and there would be no way that I'd have the time to do them and remain a police officer,' said Steele. 'To be honest, I'm not really into the reality stuff but there'll be more series documentaries as well and they are what really interests me.'

'What kind of documentaries?' asked Ronald.

'I am afraid I can't tell you.'

'Can't tell us?' said Blizzard. 'What kind of talk is that?'

'The television world is very competitive and they like to keep things under wraps until contracts have been signed.'

'Is it anything to do with Hafton?' asked Ronald. 'Because if it was, we'd have to know.'

'Not directly.'

'What does that mean?' asked Blizzard.

'Look, I really can't say,' replied Steele. 'And please don't push me on it. I'll tell you what I can when the time is right. Suffice to say that if everything comes together, it could be a whole new career for me. It's very exciting.'

Blizzard gave him a hard look; something told him that the sergeant may have uttered the words but did not completely believe what he was saying.

'Do you really want to give up your work here for something like that, just when we're getting somewhere with Javelin?' asked the inspector. He glanced at Ronald. 'The chief has already suggested that you may wish to go for Inspector at the next round of promotions, hasn't he, Arthur?'

Ronald nodded.

'I appreciate his faith in me,' said Steele. 'And yours. But I've been a police officer for seventeen years and it's time for a new challenge, one where toerags do not threaten to kill me.'

'Is that what this is about?' said Blizzard. 'You know that it's all hot air, Alan. I mean, it's not as if it's the first time you've had something like that, is it?'

'Maybe not, guv, but it gets to you in the end. Besides, if I was given this job, I'd be able to see more of Claire and the kids. I'm missing them growing up with all the hours I'm spending on Javelin.'

Blizzard gave a slight nod; since he had become a father, he had found himself more sympathetic to the needs of colleagues who were parents.

'Maybe we can do something to reduce your hours,' he said. The inspector glanced at Ronald. 'I'm sure we could sort something out.'

Ronald nodded.

'I appreciate the offer,' said Steele. 'But you know as well as I do that to do this job properly, you need to give it everything. Besides, I'm tempted by the new job.'

Blizzard scowled.

'Well, you needn't think that I'm going to take my little lad to see you in panto,' he said.

The comment defused the tension in the room and Steele was still chuckling at the joke when he arrived back in the CID office, where fellow sergeant David Colley was putting on his coat.

'And what's tickled your fancy, pray?' asked Colley.

'Just something Blizzard said.'

Colley tapped his ear a couple of times.

'Sorry,' he said. 'My hearing has been playing up. I could have sworn you said that Blizzard said something funny.'

'I'm not sure he meant it to be funny, but it was,' said Steele. He took his coat down from the peg. 'You knocking off?'

'Yeah, it's Laura's first parents' evening and I told Jay that I'd be there.'

'I'll walk out with you.'

They walked along the corridor in companionable silence, which was broken by Colley.

'Did you tell Blizzard about the telly job?' he asked.

'I did, yeah.'

'How'd it go down?'

'As you'd expect,' said Steele. 'The super was pretty reasonable about it, mind.'

'So you're serious about it then?'

'I think so,' said Steele. He pushed his way through the door leading to the station yard. 'Opportunities like this don't come along every day, do they?'

'I suppose not,' said Colley as they approached their cars. 'And who knows, you could end up on *Love Island*!'

'Somehow, I think not,' said Steele with a wry smile. 'See you tomorrow.'

But he didn't. Three hours after he had bid farewell to his colleague, Steele found himself entering a derelict warehouse down by the river.

'You there?' he shouted into the darkness.

The beam from his torch illuminated a figure as it emerged from the shadows and pointed a handgun at him.

'What the…?' exclaimed the sergeant.

'Get down on your knees.'

Steele did not move as he stared at the gun.

'If this is a joke, it's not a very–' he began.

'It's no joke.' There was a menacing edge to the voice. 'And I said get down on your knees.'

Steele did as he was told.

'I don't understand,' he said, trying in vain to conceal the fear he was feeling. 'What's this about?'

'You know exactly what it's about.'

'Surely, you don't mean…?'

He did not finish the sentence as a single gunshot reverberated around the warehouse, then all was silent.

# Chapter two

Blizzard had only just drifted off to sleep that night when the insistent ringing of the bedside phone woke him from his slumber. Never a good sleeper, the inspector had already lain in bed for the best part of an hour, turning the conversation with Alan Steele over and over his mind as he listened to Fee's rhythmic breathing and tried, as so often, not to resent his girlfriend's ability to fall asleep within minutes of her head hitting the pillow. Now, she gave a groan of protest and pulled the covers up over her head.

'If this wakes Mikey up…' she said.

They both lay and listened for a sound from the toddler's bedroom but heard nothing and, as Blizzard reached for the phone, he glanced at the digital clock's luminous readout and sighed: 12.25am. A call at that time of night was going to be bad news. The inspector picked up the phone with a deep sense of foreboding.

'Blizzard,' he grunted.

'Sorry to ring at such an hour,' said a voice he recognised as David Colley. 'But Claire Steele has been onto Control, going frantic. Alan's missing.'

Blizzard sat up in bed.

'Missing?' he said. 'What do you mean?'

'He always tells her if he's going to be late but when it got to midnight and she still hadn't heard from him, she tried his mobile and it's switched off so she rang us. She's convinced herself that something has happened to him. She's always been a bit of a worrier, has Claire, but I thought you'd want to know.'

'You're right, I do,' said Blizzard. 'He was not working on anything special tonight, was he?'

'Not as far as I'm aware. The last I saw of him was when he left the office with me just after six o'clock and he didn't mention anything.'

'Did he seem OK?'

'Seemed alright. He was a bit concerned about how you'd taken this television business but that was all,' said the sergeant. 'What do you want to do? Start a search or leave it until the morning?'

'I think we should start a search. There's probably nothing to worry about but we can't afford to take any chances.' Blizzard could hear a car engine in the background. 'I take it that you're on the way into the factory?'

'I am, yes. I'll be there in five minutes.'

'Then see if you can rustle up some bodies, will you? But keep it low profile. No helicopters or anything like that. The last thing we need is a media circus before we know what we're dealing with. I'll be in as soon as I can.'

'Righto,' said the sergeant. 'See you soon.'

The inspector replaced the receiver and flicked on the bedside light. Fee groaned again.

'Sorry, love,' he said. 'I'm going to have to go in.'

'Why, what's happened?' asked Fee. Her shock of short blonde hair finally emerged from under the blanket as she watched him getting out of bed. A former detective with Western CID, she understood only too well the demands of the job. 'A murder?'

'I do hope not,' said Blizzard. He padded across the room towards the landing. 'Alan Steele's gone AWOL.'

'That's not like him. He always tells Claire where he is.'

'I know he does. Hopefully, it'll be nothing and I'll be back in time to give Mikey his breakfast.'

'Hopefully,' said Fee.

She disappeared beneath the duvet again, leaving Blizzard to freshen up and dress hurriedly before leaving their detached house in one of the villages scattered across the rural flatlands to the west of Hafton. It took the inspector fifteen minutes to reach the outskirts of the city and, as he guided his vehicle through deserted neighbourhoods, he tried not to imagine the worst-case scenario. It was not easy to do: it was always a major cause for concern when a police officer went missing, particularly one who had received threats from the criminal fraternity, as had increasingly happened to Alan Steele as the television programme drew attention to the force's success against drug dealers. The sergeant had always tried to make light of the threats but Blizzard suspected that he was more concerned than he was prepared to admit.

Experiencing a growing sense of foreboding, the inspector turned the car onto Abbey Road and headed for the police station. His mind honed in on the episode of *Arrested!* that he had watched in Arthur Ronald's office the previous afternoon. If something *had* happened to Steele, they had a prime suspect.

Having parked his car, Blizzard headed for the CID squad room where Colley was briefing a small group of uniformed officers. Surveying the sergeant's smart appearance, the inspector felt acutely conscious that, despite the hour, Colley looked altogether more presentable than the unshaven inspector, whose hair was even more tousled than usual. Ten years younger than Blizzard, David Colley's round, almost boyish, face showed no signs of stubble and his short black hair was neatly combed. His trousers, shirt and jacket had all been perfectly ironed and his shoes shone.

Breaking away from his briefing, Colley noticed the inspector straighten his tie and chuckled.

'Much better,' he said. 'You look lovely.'

'Cheeky git,' said Blizzard ruefully. He sat down at one of the desks. 'What have we got then?'

'Not a lot,' said the sergeant. 'I've tried Alan's mobile but it's still switched off.'

Blizzard looked at the officers gathered in the room.

'So how are we going to do the search?' he asked.

'Uniform are going to start with a general sweep of this area to see if they can spot his car,' said Colley. 'Mind, without knowing where we're supposed to be looking, it's a needle in a haystack job.'

'Ah, well, I may be able to narrow it down a little,' said a plainclothes officer with short-cropped brown hair, who had just entered the room. Detective Inspector Chris Ramsey held up a piece of paper. 'I found this in Alan's top drawer. It came in this afternoon. It's a tip-off about another drugs house on the same estate as Rivermead Avenue.'

'Do we know where the information came from?' asked Blizzard.

'Crimestoppers. Anonymous caller but he mentioned Alan by name so they passed it on to him. I'm wondering if he went to check it out on his way home.'

'He didn't mention anything to me,' said Colley. 'And he would normally let one of us know if he was going to do something like that on his own.'

Ramsey did not reply.

'What are you thinking?' asked Blizzard.

'I don't want to be a scaremonger but what if it was a set-up?'

'Set up by whom?' asked Blizzard.

'Well, I was watching that episode of the reality show,' said Ramsey, 'and one of the Rivermead Avenue lads was really letting his mouth go when Alan brought him in. Threatening to kill him. A lad called Carl Latheran.'

'Yeah, I saw that,' said Blizzard. 'What do we know about him?'

'Not much really,' said Ramsey. 'We'd not encountered him or his pal before the tip-off to say that they were dealing drugs. However, judging from the footage taken in the custody suite, he seems to be a real hot-head.'

'Yes, but it was nothing that we haven't heard a thousand times before, was it?' said Colley. 'I mean, if I had a quid for every time some toerag threatened me, I'd be a rich man. Besides, Latheran and his pal are inside, aren't they?'

'Yeah, they were remanded in custody,' said Ramsey. 'They're due back in court on the twenty-fourth for sentencing.'

'Well, we need to get over to Hafton Prison to see them,' said Blizzard. 'Find out if they have been talking to anyone on the outside. David, can you sort that?'

'Sure,' said Colley. 'But I would have thought that something like this is way out of their league.'

'We need to check them out anyway,' said Blizzard. 'And we need to check out the house mentioned in the tip-off from Crimestoppers as well. You're right, though, I can't see Alan having gone to check it out on his own without telling anyone.'

'And there's no way he would have done anything until he'd gone through make-up,' said Colley with a deadpan expression on his face.

Despite their unease at Steele's disappearance, the others smiled. As ever, they appreciated the sergeant's knack of using humour to ease tense situations.

'What's the address, Chris?' asked Blizzard.

'Tennyson Avenue.'

'Go wake them up,' said the inspector.

A slim, dark-haired young woman in her twenties entered the squad room. Detective Constable Sarah Allatt was the CID department's most recent recruit.

'Just the person,' said Blizzard. 'You know Claire Steele pretty well, don't you?'

'We went to school together.'

'Excellent,' said Blizzard. He stood up. 'Can you come with me to see her, please? We need to see if she can cast some light on Alan's disappearance.'

## Chapter three

Blizzard guided his car out of the police station yard and onto a deserted Abbey Road, where the only movement was a fox rooting among a pile of pizza boxes next to a group of wheelie bins. As the inspector turned the vehicle in the direction of the city centre, he glanced across at Allatt.

'I don't really know Claire,' he said. 'You said that you were at school with her?'

'I was, yes. In fact, there was a time when it looked like we would both join the police but she ended up working at a travel agents instead.'

'But you've kept in touch?'

'We go out for the odd drink.'

'So, what's she like?' asked Blizzard. 'David reckons that she's a bit of a worrier?'

'That's a good word to describe her and I'm not surprised to hear that she's panicking about Alan. She's never come to terms with his job. I blame the constable we met at a careers fair just before we left sixth form.'

'What on earth has he got to do with it?' asked Blizzard.

'He laid it on thick about how dangerous the job can be. I reckon he was trying to impress all those teenage girls in short skirts, make it sound glamorous, big himself up, but all he did was scare the living daylights out of Claire. The next morning, she announced that there was no way that she was joining the police force.'

'So I guess she was not that impressed when she started dating Alan and found out that he was a cop?'

'She wasn't. It was a few years later but, if anything, she had grown worse. He told her on their third date and it took him ages to persuade her to go out with him again. Even now, he never tells her if he's been in danger.'

'Let's hope she does not see the new television series then,' said Blizzard. 'One of the episodes includes him receiving a death threat.'

'So I hear. She never watches the programme and Alan has been wondering how to tell her before the show airs and someone else tells her.'

'Is that why he's so keen on this new job?' asked Blizzard. He turned the car into a terraced street on the fringes of the city centre. 'To stop Claire worrying?'

'He hasn't said as much, but I suspect so. He loves being a detective, does Alan, but he loves Claire more.'

'Well, I'm afraid that I'm going to have to mention the death threat to her.' Blizzard brought the car to a halt outside one of the terraced houses and gave a slight smile. 'As you have probably noticed, Constable, sensitivity is not my strong suit so I'm relying on you to keep me right.'

'I'll do my best,' said Allatt.

Soon the detectives were sitting in the living room, surveying the slight, blonde woman who sat on the sofa and kept dabbing eyes that were red-rimmed with crying with a handkerchief.

'I know what you're thinking,' she said in a quiet voice. 'That I'm overreacting, but this is not like him, it really isn't.'

'You did the right thing in calling us,' said Blizzard. 'Better to be safe than sorry, Claire. Had he been worried about anything lately? Something at work, perhaps?'

'Why do you ask?' replied Claire anxiously. 'Has something happened? I know that he doesn't tell me everything.'

'I don't want you to read too much into this,' said Blizzard, 'but a drug dealer threatened to kill him a few weeks back. It's going to be shown in the first episode of the new series of *Community Fightback*.'

'Oh, God,' she said and put a hand to her mouth. She seemed close to tears once more.

'We're pretty sure that it was all talk,' said Blizzard quickly. He glanced at Allatt. 'It's probably nothing to do with his disappearance. Isn't that right, Constable?'

'I'm sure you're right, sir,' said Allatt. 'Criminals make a lot of empty threats, Claire, and we've heard nothing to suggest that Alan has come to any harm.'

'Then why mention it?' said Claire. She gave Blizzard a hard look. 'And Alan *is* missing, isn't he? I mean, it's hardly likely to be a coincidence, is it?'

'We shouldn't jump to conclusions,' said Blizzard. 'There could be another reason. Can you think of anything? Something in his private life, maybe? Has he been depressed?'

'Of course he's not depressed,' said Claire. 'Why would he be depressed? Did he talk to you about this new job offer? He said he would.'

'He did, yes.'

'Well then you've seen how excited he is about it.'

Before Blizzard could reply, there was a sound at the door and a child in pyjamas appeared, rubbing her eyes.

'What's happening, Mummy?' she asked.

'Nothing, lovely,' said Claire. She walked across to her young daughter. 'Come on, let's get you back to bed.'

She took the child back upstairs and returned to the living room a few moments later. Her eyes glistened with tears.

'What do I tell the kids?' she asked.

'It's probably best that you tell them nothing for the moment,' said Blizzard. 'There's no point in worrying them until we have a better idea what's happened. We've got officers out looking for Alan and there's every chance that he'll turn up safe and…'

They heard the front door open and, eyes bright with hope, Claire ran into the hallway only to reappear a few seconds later with a dark-haired woman of a similar age. Claire could not hide her disappointment and she slumped into an armchair and the tears started to flow. The new arrival sat down next to her and put a hand round her shoulders. She looked at Allatt.

'Hi, Sarah,' she said.

'Hi, Janice,' said Allatt. The constable gestured to her boss. 'This is Detective Chief Inspector Blizzard. Guv, this is Claire's sister.'

'We were just trying to think if there is any reason why Alan would not come home,' said Blizzard. 'Has he mentioned anything to you?'

'Nothing,' said Janice. 'But then he's not the type to talk about things that are on his mind. I imagine that you're all like that, you blokes.'

'I guess we are,' said Blizzard; Fee often chided him for bottling up his feelings. He stood up. 'If you do think of anything, will you let me know? I'll send a couple of uniform officers back to do a proper search of the house in the morning. We don't want to disturb the children any more than is necessary tonight.'

'Why would you want to search the house?' asked Janice. 'Alan's not here.'

'You'd be amazed how many missing people turn up in their own homes,' said Blizzard.

When the detectives were back in the car, the inspector glanced at Allatt.

'Is there a chance that Alan has been playing away?' he asked. 'Are we sure that he's not tucked up in someone else's bed?'

'I can't see it. They're rock solid, are Alan and Claire.'

'Nevertheless, we shouldn't discount the possibility,' said Blizzard.

'But…'

'We have to treat this like any other case, Sarah,' said the inspector as he started the engine. 'We can't afford to view Alan differently just because he's one of our own.'

# Chapter four

It was just after 2am when the police smashed their way into the property on Tennyson Avenue that had been identified by the caller to Crimestoppers. Shouting their customary warnings, the officers ran up the stairs and brought down two young men. A quick search of the house came up with the usual bags of pills and rolls of money but no sign of Alan Steele, nor was any useful information gleaned from the prisoners during curt questioning by a frustrated Chris Ramsey before the duo were bundled into a waiting van and driven to Abbey Road Police Station.

Half an hour later, one of the young men was slumped in his chair in an interview room, staring insolently across the desk at a stern-faced John Blizzard. Aged in his late teens, Charlie Walters was dressed in the T-shirt and jeans that had been hurriedly thrown on following his arrest. His arms were crossed in a gesture of defiance and Blizzard sighed; the more experienced criminals in the city still regarded the prospect of being interviewed by the inspector with trepidation but that tended not to be the case with the up-and-coming generation of younger criminals. Many of them were in their teens and early twenties and behaved with a lack of respect towards the police that troubled the inspector.

Charlie Walters glanced at the clock on the wall.

'When you going to let me go?' he demanded. 'It's nearly three o'clock.'

'I am perfectly aware what time it is,' said Blizzard wearily. 'And believe me, I would much rather be in bed than talking to some snot-nosed kid who's not long out of short trousers.'

'You can't talk to me like that,' said Walters. He pointed to a force poster on the wall depicting a black teenager and an elderly white woman talking to a police officer. Printed above the image in large type was the mantra *You can expect to be treated with respect by our officers – whoever you are.*

'Listen, you little toerag,' said Blizzard angrily. He leaned forward and jabbed a finger at the prisoner. 'One of my officers is missing and I am in no mood for games.'

'Yeah, well like I keep saying, I know nothing about that,' said Walters. 'I've never even met him. All I know is what I've seen on the telly. Strutting about like he's the fucking chief constable. The man's a Grade A tosser.'

Blizzard resisted the temptation to challenge the statement; time was ticking by and there was little to be gained from an argument at such an hour. He tried a more conciliatory approach instead.

'Surely, you must have heard *something*?' he said. 'If you have, I may be tempted to go easy on you. Put a word in with the judge on your behalf when your case comes to court.'

'And you expect me to believe that? I mean, you ain't going to pretend you didn't find drugs at the house, are you? Anyway, like I told you, I don't know anything.'

There was a knock on the door and Chris Ramsey walked into the interview room.

'Anything from his pal?' asked Blizzard hopefully.

'Nothing.' Ramsey glanced at Walters. 'What about meladdo here?'

'Same.'

'Are you going to give us bail then?' said Walters.

'No bloody chance,' said Blizzard. 'I imagine that the detective inspector plans to keep you in overnight while we continue our inquiries.'

Ramsey nodded.

'In which case,' said Walters, 'I think it's time that I saw a solicitor, don't you? Get one of them fuckers out of their beds in the middle of the night.'

And the teenager sat back in his seat with the air of a man who was not going to answer any more questions.

'Get him out of my sight, Chris,' said Blizzard. 'Let's hope that he's more co-operative in the morning after trying to get to sleep on one of those mattresses.'

'At least he'll get some sleep,' grunted Ramsey and led Walters from the room.

A few minutes later, Blizzard was back in his office, sitting at his desk and moodily sipping from his mug of tea as he contemplated the lack of progress in the search for the missing detective. Arthur Ronald walked into the room and sat down heavily at the desk.

'Where *is* he?' he asked.

'God knows,' replied Blizzard.

'There's not a chance that he's killed himself, is there?'

'It seems unlikely, Arthur. There's been no suggestion that he was depressed and it seems unlikely that he's run off with another woman either.'

'Would that he had, John. It would make life considerably less complicated.' Like Blizzard, the superintendent was acutely conscious that the more time passed without hearing from the missing detective, the less chance there was of finding him alive. 'I hate to say it, but it's looking more and more like foul play.'

Blizzard nodded gloomily but before he could reply, a grim-faced David Colley walked into the room.

'You don't look like a man with good news,' said Blizzard.

'I'm afraid I'm not,' replied the sergeant. 'Uniform have found Alan's car.'

'Where?'

'In that car park by the river, behind the new Tesco. There's no sign of Alan, though. I said that we'd meet forensics down there.'

Blizzard glanced at the wall clock, stood up and reached for his coat.

'Come on then,' he said with a sigh. 'At this rate, I'll be back just in time to give Mikey his breakfast.'

'Optimist,' said Colley as they headed out into the corridor. 'And don't pretend that you don't like your daily dose of *Thomas the Tank Engine*. You should count yourself lucky, anyway, all Laura watches at the moment is *My Little Pony*. It's enough to melt your brain. Can we go in separate cars? I've arranged to see those lads at the prison afterwards.'

It did not take the detectives long to drive to the supermarket, where they turned off the dual carriageway and followed a dirt track that wound its way through an area of wasteland until it reached a wooded car park on the banks of the River Haft. Forensics officers in white overalls were already setting up an arc light to allow them to examine Alan Steele's vehicle and, while Blizzard waited for the initial results, he wandered off towards the shingle shoreline to gather thoughts that were growing ever darker.

It was a place that the inspector knew well, somewhere that he often visited to relax his turbulent mind during difficult investigations. However, there were no such calming thoughts on this occasion as he stood and gazed across towards the lights of the chemical complex on the south bank and listened to the lapping of the water. The presence of Alan Steele's vehicle in the car park felt like the violation of a special place and Blizzard was filled with a deepening sense of foreboding.

Someone called his name and he headed back to the car park where one of the forensics officers had slipped out of his overalls to reveal wavy brown hair, a smart grey suit with a red silk tie and shiny black shoes. Detective Inspector Graham Ross, the head of forensics in Western Division, was the most sartorially elegant of all the officers at Abbey Road and, instinctively, Blizzard reached up to straighten his tie. Ross noticed the gesture and gave a slight smile.

'It'll take more than that,' he said.

'Yes, thank you, Versace,' replied Blizzard. He cursed inwardly that the gesture had been spotted. The inspector gestured towards the car. 'You got anything useful to say?'

'We've found nothing in the car that points to foul play and I don't think it was stolen. I reckon it was parked, rather than abandoned.' Ross glanced towards the dark and brooding waters of the river. 'I've got this awful feeling that he may be in there.'

'Right little ray of sunshine, aren't you?' said Blizzard.

'We're all thinking it.'

Blizzard sighed.

'You're right,' he said. 'We are.'

# Chapter five

Daylight was breaking as David Colley left the bypass that cut through the east side of the city and brought his vehicle to a halt in the deserted Hafton Prison car park. As always when the sergeant visited the prison, he sat in his vehicle for a few moments and surveyed the bleak red-brick frontage. As he did so, he experienced the same thought as on previous occasions, that, surely, no one who had spent any time at the infernal place would wish to go through the experience again. However, it never failed to amaze him that so many repeat offenders were to be found among its population, including a number that he had arrested.

The thought strengthened as he entered the building, just as it always did. Constructed in the Victorian age, Hafton Prison had undergone little in the way of modernisation and was dark, overcrowded and pervaded by stale air that stank of sweat. It all made for an oppressive atmosphere and the sergeant detested his visits. Having gone through the security process with the unsmiling guards, he was led to an interview room where two teenage inmates were waiting, watched over by a stern-faced prison officer who stood by the door with his arms crossed. The teenagers, both of whom Colley recognised from the television programme's coverage of the raid on Rivermead Avenue several weeks previously, viewed the sergeant with little enthusiasm as he took his seat at the table.

'Which one of you is Carl Latheran?' he asked.

One of the boys, a skinny, unshaven young man with bad skin and straggly dark hair, wafted a hand lazily. Despite his young age, he had the air of someone who was at home in prison. Colley turned his attention to the other boy, similarly wiry but altogether better turned out, clean-shaven with neatly cropped short blond hair. Unlike Carl Latheran, he did not look like he belonged in prison; there was a nervousness about his demeanour.

'So, you must be Edward Janes?' said the sergeant.

The young man nodded.

'Brilliant,' said Latheran, glancing at his accomplice. 'That's why he was made up to detective, you know. They'll be giving him his own TV show next – like that copper that arrested us. Mind, the only show that you lot will get a part in is *The Muppets*.'

The teenager grinned delightedly at his joke and, despite his unease at the situation in which he found himself, Janes allowed himself a smile as well. Colley sighed; he agreed with Blizzard that there was a worrying lack of respect for the police among the young up-and-coming generation of criminals. Before the sergeant could utter a retort, the prison officer gave Latheran a hard look.

'Watch your mouth,' he growled. 'And answer his questions.'

'He hasn't asked any,' said Latheran. 'What's he here about, anyway? We're missing our breakfast because of this.'

'I am investigating the disappearance of Detective Sergeant Steele,' said Colley.

'What do you mean "disappearance"?' asked Latheran. The grin vanished and he was suddenly wary.

'Just what I said. He hasn't been seen since just gone six yesterday.'

'Well, that's got nowt to do with us,' said Latheran. The teenager tried to sound casual. 'And don't you try and say it is, neither.'

'Are you sure you don't know anything about it?' said Colley. 'You mentioned him before you even knew why I was here. That's pretty suspicious, wouldn't you say? And when you were arrested, you did threaten to kill him.'

'Hey, don't try to pin this on me,' said Latheran quickly. 'It was just talk in the heat of the moment. Besides, how could we do anything about it anyway? In case you haven't noticed, we've been here since we were nicked.'

'You could have got one of your pals on the outside to do it.'

'There's no way we could have organised anything like that,' said Janes. Like Latheran, he was looking increasingly alarmed at the way the interview was going. 'It's way out of our league.'

Colley surveyed him for a few moments. He was tempted to believe them and, after a few more minutes of questioning which did nothing to make him think otherwise, the sergeant ended the interview and left the prison, revelling in the fresh breeze that was blowing in off the river. As he walked across the car park, he was suddenly aware of how tired he was.

# Chapter six

An equally weary John Blizzard went home shortly after 6.30am and gave his son his breakfast of toast, fruit and yoghurt in front of an episode of *Thomas the Tank Engine* before heading upstairs to grab a couple of hours' sleep. He groaned in protest when he was roused from slumber by Fee gently shaking his shoulder.

'Sorry to wake you,' she said. 'But we're off. Do you want to say goodbye to Mikey?'

'Is it that time already?' he mumbled.

'I'm afraid so.'

The inspector glanced blearily at the bedside digital clock, groaned again and forced himself out of bed, wincing at a sudden stab of pain from his bad back. He stood still for a couple of seconds to allow the pain to subside before gingerly starting to walk across the bedroom again.

'Take your time, Grandad,' said Fee.

Blizzard, who was acutely aware of the age difference between them, gave her a withering look but Fee knew that he viewed the comment in the manner in which it was intended. She left the room and, as Blizzard passed the dressing table, he stopped to unplug his mobile phone from its charger. There had not been any calls but he guessed that it would not be long before it rang; he was surprised that it had not done so already.

Feeling horribly thick-headed, he stumbled down the stairs and into the hall where Fee was preparing to leave the house in order to drop their son off at the childminder before heading for her job with a city centre security company. Blizzard kissed the child and made to do the same with his girlfriend but she took one look at his unshaven features and shook her head.

'No thank you,' she said. 'And make sure you shave before you go back in. You look like something the cat dragged in.'

'Yes, thank you for those few kind words,' murmured Blizzard.

Fee grinned and carried Mikey to her vehicle. The toddler waved cheerily back at his father and Blizzard stood on the doorstep, waving back at his son. As he was watching Fee strap the child into the car seat, the inspector's mobile phone rang. It was Chris Ramsey and the smile faded.

'Have you found him?' asked Blizzard, taking the call.

'Not yet,' said the detective inspector. 'But you might want to get down to the search site. We've got a bit of a situation developing.'

'What kind of situation?'

'The *Community Fightback* crew are here,' said Ramsey. 'They're demanding to film the search for Alan.'

'Well, tell them they can't,' said Blizzard. He waved at Fee as she reversed the car out of the drive. 'Tell them that I will not allow it.'

'I think it may have to come from you,' said Ramsey. 'They won't listen to me. They say it's their right to film wherever they want. You know what they're like.'

'That's all we need,' said the inspector with a sigh. 'I'll be there as quickly as I can. Don't let them in until I get there.'

After taking a quick shower and wolfing down a couple of slices of toast, the inspector headed into Hafton, driving one-handed as he shaved with his electric razor while negotiating the morning rush-hour traffic. Arriving at the site, he parked his vehicle and stood for a few moments to watch a line of uniformed officers working their way painstakingly across the wasteland between the new supermarket and the riverbank. The inspector noticed that several more officers were checking the row of derelict warehouses down by the jetty. Having once been used by fruit importers, they had closed one by one to remain as grim reminders of the recession that hit the city following the financial crash of 2008.

Blizzard strode across to where Chris Ramsey was standing with a young woman whose tumbling red hair was jammed beneath a cap that bore the image of a revolver and the motto *Smoking Gun Films*, the name of the company making *Arrested! Community Fightback*. She was with a young man who held a camera and both looked frustrated. The detective inspector turned towards his boss with a relieved look on his face.

'Boy, am I glad you're here,' he said. 'I've told them that it would not be appropriate to film the search but they won't take no for an answer.'

'Is that right?' said Blizzard. His tone of voice suggested that after two hours' sleep, he was not in the mood for dissent. It was not the first time that he and Sally Jackson, the series producer and a director of Smoking Gun Films, had exchanged harsh words and there was no love lost between them.

'Our agreement says that we can film whatever we want,' she said. 'And that means that we can be with your search teams.'

'My understanding is that your agreement covers our raids on drug suppliers as part of Operation Javelin,' said Blizzard. 'This falls outside that.'

'Except that Alan Steele heads up Javelin, which means that we have every right to film the search.'

'How did you find out what was happening anyway?' asked Blizzard suspiciously. 'We haven't released anything to the media yet.'

'We were due to film some general shots with Alan this morning and when he didn't answer his mobile, we rang the station and they told us what had happened. You should really have called us last night.'

'I don't see why,' said Blizzard, bridling at the accusatory tone of the comment. 'And in case you hadn't noticed, I don't work for you and I'm not at your beck and call.'

'But it's a dramatic twist to the story,' said Bob Harrold, the cameraman. 'It could make for a really strong episode all on its own. The footage would be really powerful.'

'Stuff that!' exclaimed Blizzard angrily. 'One of my officers is missing. One with a wife and two young kids. That's what matters here, not your blessed television series.'

'Yes but…' began the cameraman.

Blizzard looked across to a couple of young, uniformed officers who were standing on the edge of the car park watching the confrontation.

'Here, you two,' he shouted. 'Do something useful. Get these jokers out of here.'

The officers moved towards the film crew.

'If you do that, there'll be big trouble,' said Jackson. 'You'll have to explain yourself to the chief constable.'

'I've spent a career doing that,' said Blizzard. He gestured to the young officers, who had hesitated. 'Go on, get on with it.'

One of the officers took the producer by the arm and started to lead her away. She shrugged herself free and glared at Blizzard.

'This is a disgrace!' she exclaimed. 'We deserve more respect.'

Blizzard gave a thin smile.

'In which case,' he said, looking at the uniformed officers again, 'would you *respectfully* get them out of here, please?'

Ramsey watched the officers as they led the protesting film crew away.

'There'll be hell to pay for that,' he said. 'She's a hard-headed woman, is Sally Jackson. She already acts like she owns the place and she's got the chief wrapped round her little finger.'

'Yes, well, the last thing we want is them filming if, God forbid, we do find a body.' Blizzard looked back towards the officers searching the wasteland. 'So where are we with this?'

'They've just started on the warehouses. We'd have been in there earlier but they're deathtraps and I've spent half my time this morning filling in health and safety forms to keep HR happy.'

'I'll bet you have,' said Blizzard. He headed back towards his car. 'Keep me informed.'

'Will do. Where will you be?'

'I'm going back to see Claire Steele. See if she's thought of anything that might explain where her husband is.'

Blizzard noticed a Sky News vehicle heading along the bypass towards the edge of the wasteland.

'It looks like the media have cottoned on to what's happening,' he said. 'Tell uniform that I want them all kept well away from the search.'

'What do you want me to do if they insist?' asked Ramsey.

Blizzard gestured towards a young woman standing on the edge of the wasteland, deep in conversation on her mobile phone.

'Tell them to talk to Marie,' he said. 'It's the press office's problem. They can sort it out.'

* * *

Twenty minutes later, the inspector had just reached out to ring the bell at the Steeles' house when the door was opened by Sarah Allatt.

'Morning, guv,' said the detective constable, standing aside to let her boss in.

'Morning, Sarah,' said Blizzard. Still feeling fuzzy-headed, the inspector marvelled yet again at how young officers always appeared to be so fresh and full of energy despite being short of sleep. His back gave a twinge as if to remind him that he was getting older. 'Have you been home?'

'Not yet.'

'Well make sure you get a couple of hours after this,' said Blizzard as they stood in the hallway. 'We need to keep our people as fresh as possible. How's Claire?'

'In bits,' said Allatt. 'Janice tried to persuade her to go to bed but she refused.'

Blizzard looked towards the stairs as he heard voices.

'They're still doing the search, I presume?' he said.

'They're just finishing off in the loft. They've done the rest of the house and the garden. We took the kids to a neighbour's for their breakfast and she's dropping them off at school. They don't know that their father is missing yet.'

Blizzard thought of Mikey.

'I don't envy whoever has to tell them,' he said.

A uniformed officer clumped down the stairs.

'Anything?' asked Blizzard.

'He's definitely not here,' said the officer. 'And we've found nothing to indicate where he might have gone either. No note. Nothing.'

Blizzard nodded and pushed open the door to the living room where Claire was sitting on the sofa with Janice next to her, holding her hand. They both looked up hopefully as the inspector walked in.

'Any news?' asked Janice.

Blizzard sat down in one of the armchairs.

'I am afraid not,' he said. 'We're still searching the wasteland where his car was found.'

'No news is good news, I suppose,' said Janice.

'Hopefully,' said Blizzard. The inspector decided that this was not the time to tell her that it was not a mantra to which he had ever subscribed; he'd experienced too many disappointments for him to believe it. Instead, he looked at Claire. 'Have you thought of anything that might explain why Alan was down by the river last night?'

Claire shook her head. Blizzard hesitated for a moment, seeking the right words for his next question.

'I'm sorry, but I have to ask you this,' he said. 'Is there a chance that he might have been meeting someone?'

'Like who?' asked Claire. 'Someone for his work? I told you, Alan never–'

'A woman.'

Claire's reaction surprised Blizzard. He had expected a vigorous rebuttal of the suggestion but instead she gave a slight nod of the head.

'It's possible,' she said.

Janice, who had been about to protest at the question, looked at her sister in astonishment.

'Surely, you don't believe that, do you, Claire?' she said. 'Alan dotes on you. You know that.'

'Then where is he?' said Claire. 'What if he *is* having an affair, Janice? What if I had kidded myself that he wasn't?'

'What makes you think that he might be?' asked Blizzard.

'All those late nights.'

'You can blame me for them,' said Blizzard. 'He's been putting in a lot of hours because of Operation Javelin. You know the way the job works, Claire. There's a lot to do co-ordinating an operation like that, not to mention making sure that the film crew has everything they need. They're very demanding and he's had to work closely with the producer.'

'Ah, yes, the producer,' said Claire. She gave a mirthless laugh. 'He's always had a thing about redheads, hasn't he, Janice? Remember the woman from the shoe shop?'

'That was years ago,' protested Janice.

Blizzard gave her a quizzical look.

'Alan and Claire had only just started going out but were on a break from each other,' explained Janice. 'He went out with this other woman a couple of times. It didn't come to anything and he's been faithful to Claire ever since.'

'So, what makes you think that he's been having an affair with Sally Jackson?' asked Blizzard, looking at Claire. 'And how come you did not mention this last night?'

'No woman wants to admit that her husband is having an affair,' said Claire. 'But I've had a lot of time to think since he went missing.'

'If you ask me, you've had too much time to think,' said Janice. 'And you've had no sleep, remember. That can do strange things to the mind.'

'The signs were all there,' said Claire. 'She came to the house several times and they went out for dinner. Alan said it was purely professional but he has gone out a couple of times in the past week and not told me where he's been going. He got really funny with me when I pushed him on it. Said it was better that I did not know. What if he was with her?'

'I'm not sure you're right about that,' said Blizzard. 'I've just been with her and her only interest seemed to be how much of the search they could film.'

'Well perhaps you should talk to her again. Ask the question.'

'We'll certainly check it out,' said Blizzard. He stood up and headed for the door. 'Just to be sure.'

'You do that,' said Claire.

The inspector did not speak again until he and Allatt were out in the street.

'You know those difficult questions that I said that we might have to ask?' he said.

Allatt nodded.

'Well, maybe one of them is for Claire,' said the inspector. 'Namely, where were you between six o'clock and midnight last night?'

'Surely, you're not thinking that she's involved?'

'It's one of the oldest motives in the book, Sarah,' said Blizzard. 'The betrayed wife.'

'Yes, but *Claire and Alan*?' said the constable. 'I'm sorry, guv, but there's no way I can see that being true.'

'I hope you're right,' replied the inspector. 'But I'm beginning to think that there's something we're not being told about the perfect life of Alan and Claire Steele. And the way it's looking, it could be something that cost Alan his life.'

# Chapter seven

It was a pensive John Blizzard who returned to Abbey Road Police Station and immediately called his team to the main briefing room. The passage of so many hours without a sighting of the missing detective had convinced him that something bad had happened and the inspector was experiencing a strong sense that events were running away from him. A man who had always experienced an overwhelming urge to be in control, Blizzard felt a pressing need to impose himself on the situation.

He had just walked to the front of the briefing room, watched with anticipation by the assembled detectives and uniformed officers, when a grim-faced Arthur Ronald arrived. There were a few surprised looks when the superintendent walked into the room – he tended not to attend Blizzard's briefings because he had always been careful to publicly exhibit faith in his friend's leadership of Western CID. Not attending briefings sent out a clear message that Blizzard was in control. However, there were exceptions and the events of recent hours had dictated that the superintendent be present. He gestured to his friend to join him in the corridor.

'A word before you start, please, John,' he said.

Once they were out of the room, with the door shut behind them, Blizzard surveyed the superintendent's grim expression with concern.

'Something wrong?' he asked.

'Wrong?' hissed Ronald. He was unable to conceal his exasperation with his old friend anymore. 'I'll say something's wrong. What on earth did you say to the film crew?'

'That they can't film the search for Alan.'

'And why would you say that?' demanded Ronald.

'I didn't think it would be appropriate.'

'Well, do you know how much trouble you've caused?' exclaimed Ronald. 'They're playing merry hell about it. I have told you time and time again to put aside your personal antipathy when dealing with them.'

'My dislike of them had nothing to do with it,' said Blizzard calmly. 'I was thinking of Alan's family. I don't want cameras there if we find his body. Can you imagine how upsetting that would be for Claire and the kids if it was all over the television screen? You're the one who's always telling me to be more sympathetic with victims.'

The comment mollified the superintendent's anger a little.

'Yes, well that's very commendable, I'm sure,' he said, calming down. 'Very considerate of you but the fact remains that the film company has threatened the chief with legal action for breach of contract.'

'And what did the chief tell them?' said Blizzard. 'Rolled over to have his tummy tickled, I imagine.'

'Oh, behave, man! He had no option but to agree. It's all there in black and white.' Ronald gave his friend a hard look. 'Anyway, I am to make it clear that you will offer them every assistance possible. Do you understand?'

'I do, yes, but there's something that may complicate matters. Claire Steele has got it into her head that Sally Jackson has been having an affair with Alan.'

'That's all we need,' said Ronald. 'Do you believe her?'

'I'm not sure.'

'Well, tread carefully,' said Ronald. 'If it's wrong and it gets out, it could be very damaging. Sally is a tough cookie. Not one to cross.'

Blizzard was about to remind his friend that neither was he but they both heard the buzz of conversation suddenly grow louder through the closed briefing room door.

'You'd better get in there,' said Ronald. 'We don't want to keep folks waiting too long. Is it OK if I sit in? The chief is demanding updates every twenty minutes.'

Blizzard nodded and went back into the briefing room where he stood at the front while Ronald took a seat at the back. The inspector held up a hand and the room fell silent.

'Thank you for your attendance, ladies and gentlemen,' he said. 'I appreciate that many of you have been up all night.'

The inspector turned to the noticeboard behind him, onto which had been pinned a picture of the missing detective. Blizzard looked at Colley, who was in his customary position leaning against a wall.

'We know that Alan left here at six o'clock last night with David,' said the inspector. 'The question is what happened between them going their separate ways in the police station car park and Alan's vehicle arriving on the riverbank later in the evening? Any ANPR hits on his car last night, Chris?'

'Traffic say not,' said Ramsey. 'However, we ran a check with Alan's mobile phone provider and their GPS shows that he was at the McDonald's in the Batley Road Retail Park when he switched the phone off just after 7.30, which has thrown up a bit of mystery.'

'What kind of a mystery?' asked Blizzard.

Ramsey nodded at a middle-aged woman with short dark hair, who was sitting in the front row. Detective Constable Jenny Carr was another recent recruit to

Western CID and had been transferred in response to Blizzard's request for a more experienced officer following the arrival of several younger detectives.

'I've just got back from Batley Road,' she said. 'One of the staff recognised Alan from the television and says that he had a meal in the restaurant then sat in his car, talking on his mobile for a good twenty minutes before driving off at 8.15. Their CCTV has confirmed that.'

'So, given that he switched his mobile off at 7.30, that means he has two phones?' said Blizzard.

'If he did, the mobile phone company does not have a record of the second one,' said Carr. 'We're checking other phone providers but nothing so far.'

Blizzard turned back to the noticeboard and tapped the pictures of four young men that had been pinned up below the image of Alan Steele.

'And where do our teenage drug dealers fit into things?' he said. '*Do* they fit into things? Is this anything to do with Operation Javelin or not?'

'Alan has overseen a lot of arrests,' said Ramsey, 'but I reckon we can discount the two we arrested in Tennyson Avenue last night. There's nothing to suggest that Alan had done anything about the Crimestoppers tip-off. If his disappearance is to do with Javelin, I'd say that Charlie Walters is a much better option. He *was* filmed threatening to kill Alan, after all. Dave doesn't agree, though.'

Ramsey glanced at Colley.

'Do you?' he said.

'Not really,' said the sergeant. 'I have just come back from seeing him and his pal in prison and Walters says that the threat was all hot air, him shooting his mouth off. I'm tempted to agree; conspiracy to murder is way out of their league. Besides, their only visitors since they were locked up have been family members, none of whom have criminal records.'

'It doesn't have to be arranged through family members, though,' said Ramsey. 'They could have been talking to someone on the outside on a mobile. Hafton Prison's got a real problem with them being smuggled in.'

'Except the prison officers swear that neither Walters nor his pal have one,' said Colley. 'Their cells have been searched several times since they were banged up. I think we could end up wasting a lot of time on Charlie Walters.'

Silence settled on the room as Blizzard hesitated for a few moments, wondering how best to phrase his next comment.

'What about Claire?' he asked eventually.

'What about her?' asked Ramsey. He seemed taken aback by the question and a number of other officers looked at their boss with surprise. 'Surely, you don't think that she could have anything to do with this?'

'I'm just asking the question, Chris.'

'And why would you do that?' asked Ramsey.

'Because Claire thinks that Alan has been having an affair with one of the women on the film crew. Sally Jackson.'

'Alan having an affair?' said Ramsey. He shook his head. 'I can't see that. He's devoted to Claire.'

He looked round the room for support and several officers nodded their agreement. Sitting at the back of the room, Arthur Ronald frowned but said nothing.

'Devoted or not,' said Blizzard, 'Claire has convinced herself that Alan has been playing away. It doesn't need to be true. What matters is that she believes it and if something *has* happened to Alan, that's something that we can't ignore.'

Ramsey was about to reply when a visibly upset uniformed officer entered the briefing room.

'Sorry to interrupt,' he said, 'but the search team have found him.'

# Chapter eight

It was with a tight knot forming in the pit of his stomach that John Blizzard got out of his car and made his way across the wasteland towards the derelict warehouses. Blizzard had lost officers under his command before and as he walked he recalled their faces; two young detective constables killed in a road accident during a surveillance operation run by the drugs squad on the city's east side, and a fresh-faced, young uniformed constable who died not long after Blizzard took charge of Western CID. The inspector had organised a raid on a notorious housing estate, during which the constable was stabbed to death in the stairwell of a block of flats.

Memories of that wicked night came back to the inspector as he walked and Blizzard recalled how each death had sent shockwaves through the force. They were like deaths in the family, the loss of one of their own, and each time it happened, the sense of bereavement cast a long shadow. Blizzard knew that it would be the same this time and that a key part of his job would be managing staff morale in the days and weeks to come.

A small group of uniformed officers had gathered in solemn silence by the main door of the nearest warehouse and Blizzard walked up to the inspector who had been co-ordinating the search.

'Is it definitely him?' he asked.

'I'm afraid so,' she said. 'He's inside.'

Blizzard was about to enter the building when he noticed Chris Ramsey approaching across the wasteland, accompanied by the television company producer Sally Jackson and Bob Harrold, the cameraman. They appeared to be involved in an animated conversation.

'That's all we need,' said Blizzard.

'Tell me about it,' said the uniformed inspector. 'They've been making a pest of themselves all morning. I was told to let them get plenty of footage of the search but we can't let them film the body, surely?'

'Not if I have anything to do with it,' said Blizzard.

'But *have* you got anything to do with it? I heard that the chief got heavy about it and ordered you to let them do whatever they want.'

Blizzard frowned; his achievements as a commanding officer were largely based on his reputation as a no-nonsense policeman who was in control of situations and he hated the damage that could be caused by loss of face.

'We'll see,' he said. He turned to meet the producer and cameraman. 'Miss Jackson, what a surprise.'

'Have you found him?' she asked.

'I'm not at liberty to–'

'Because that's what we've heard; that he's in the warehouse. And if you have found him, we'd like to do some filming in there.'

'All in good time,' said Blizzard.

'But the chief con–'

'Look,' said Blizzard, trying to sound conciliatory, 'I've only just arrived myself and I need to check it out first. If you'd wait here for a few minutes, I'll see what I can do.'

As Blizzard turned towards the warehouse, Bob Harrold took a step to follow him but Chris Ramsey blocked his way.

'Oi!' exclaimed the cameraman.

'He said wait a few minutes,' said the detective inspector.

Harrold tried to push past him.

'Just show some humanity, will you!' exclaimed Ramsey. 'That's one of our own in there! One of our friends.'

Sally Jackson gave the cameraman a sharp look and he stopped his efforts to get past the detective inspector.

'We're sorry,' she said. The tone of her voice was less confrontational. 'We were forgetting ourselves.'

Blizzard gave a nod of appreciation.

'You'll get your opportunity to film in the warehouse,' he said. 'I promise. And at some stage, we'll need to talk to your team as well.'

'Why?' asked Jackson.

'Because they may have picked up some useful information,' said Blizzard. He had decided not to broach the rumour about an affair for the moment but searched the producer's face for an indication that she might be concealing something. He found nothing. 'Now, if you'd wait here, that would be appreciated.'

Producer and cameraman moved away and the uniformed inspector pushed open the door to the warehouse, which creaked loudly as she led the way into the cavernous interior of the building, followed by Blizzard and Ramsey. The air was heavy with the lingering stench of years of decay and pigeon droppings and Blizzard felt it catch, sharp and rank, at the back of his throat. The only light filtered through gaping holes in the roof and it took the officers' eyes a few moments to adapt to the gloom.

'What a place to die,' murmured Blizzard.

The uniformed inspector led the detectives to the far end of the warehouse where Alan Steele's body was sprawled on the floor next to a pile of overturned, rusty, metal shelving. The detectives could clearly see the cause of death – a single bullet hole in the middle of the forehead. Neat. Clinical. Fatal. Ramsey gave Blizzard a shocked look.

'That's an execution,' he said. 'A professional job.'

'And way beyond the kind of people that he's been dealing with as part of Javelin,' said Blizzard. 'Everyone we've nicked has been small-time or middle-level dealers. I can't see any of them having the wherewithal to hire a professional hitman. Can you?'

Before Ramsey could reply, the creaking of the door heralded the arrival of DI Graham Ross. Already wearing his white overalls, he walked up to the gathering and stared down into the sergeant's bloodless face. After regaining his composure, he glanced at the others and made an effort to maintain a detached demeanour and come over as professional. However, the tremor in his voice betrayed the strong emotions he was experiencing.

'If you plan on staying here, can I ask you to put on some overalls, please?' he said. 'We need to preserve the scene.'

'Sorry,' said Blizzard. 'We'll leave you to get on with it. Let me know what you find.'

Ross gestured to the remainder of his team, who were standing by the door and now began walking towards their boss. Blizzard and Ramsey went back outside, relieved to be back in the bright sunlight.

'This was definitely a set-up,' said Blizzard. 'We need to find out who Alan was talking to on his mobile outside McDonald's last night, as a matter of urgency. They're the main suspect.'

'I'll chase it up,' said Ramsey.

Blizzard detected weariness in his voice.

'Not until you've grabbed some sleep, you won't,' he said.

'Don't worry about me, I'll be alright.'

'Go home and get some sleep,' repeated Blizzard. 'That's an order No one will think any less of you for it. I'll ask David to oversee things at the factory for a couple of hours. I've got to drop into Abbey Road to pick Sarah up before we go and break the news to Claire anyway.'

'I don't envy you that job,' said Ramsey.

'No, neither do I,' said Blizzard.

He walked over to the uniformed inspector.

'I need to have a quick word with the TV people, then can you let them into the warehouse, please?' he said. 'You can give them some uniformed officers to make it look good but no shots of the body.'

The inspector nodded.

'Understood,' she said.

Blizzard walked over to Sally Jackson, who was standing on her own while the cameraman filmed shots of officers outside the warehouse.

'Is it him?' she asked.

'I'm afraid so but keep it to yourself. His wife doesn't know yet.'

'Of course,' said Jackson. 'Poor woman.'

Blizzard glanced round to make sure that he could not be overheard.

'Look,' he said in a low voice, 'there's a rumour that you have been having an affair with Alan. Is there any truth to it?'

'Who told you that?' she said sharply.

'Never mind who told me. Is it true?'

'Of course not!' exclaimed Jackson. Anger flashed in her eyes. 'There's no way I would have an affair with anyone I work with and my relationship with Alan was purely professional. Even if I wanted to have a relationship with someone, I work far too many hours for it to ever succeed.'

To the inspector, it appeared to be a genuine reaction and he did not sense that she was keeping anything from him.

'Fair enough…' he began. 'But–'

'What's more, I resent you suggesting that I would ever do anything like that,' she said, not giving him the chance to complete his sentence. She gave him a hard look. 'And I don't want it spreading round Abbey Road either. I know what police stations are like when it comes to gossip, you're like a bunch of old women, and something like this could be very damaging. Ten jobs depend on what I do and there's no way that I could allow anything to put them at risk.'

Blizzard held up both hands in mock-surrender.

'Message received and understood,' he said.

She stood up and gave him another look.

'Just you make sure that it is,' she said and went to rejoin the cameraman.

When she had gone, Blizzard exhaled a couple of times.

'Give me villains any day,' he murmured.

* * *

Twenty minutes later, he and Allatt arrived at Claire Steele's house and sat for a few moments in the car before Blizzard sighed and opened his door.

'Come on,' he said. 'Delaying it won't make it any easier.'

The front door was opened by Janice, who took one look at the solemn expression on the detectives' faces and instantly knew why they were there. She clapped a hand to her mouth.

'Please, God, no,' she said.

'I'm sorry,' said Blizzard. He walked into the hallway. 'Where's Claire?'

'I persuaded her to go to bed. She's been asleep for an hour or so. I'll go and wake her up.'

Blizzard nodded and the detectives made their way into the living room where they sat and waited in the heavy silence. Claire arrived a couple of minutes later, her face ashen and her eyes bloodshot. She half-collapsed onto the sofa and Janice sat next to her, holding her hand.

'How did he die?' asked Janice in a quiet voice.

'He was shot,' said Blizzard. 'I'm really sorry.'

Even as he uttered the word, he was acutely aware how hollow it sounded. It always did when confronted by such agony and the experience never got any easier, regardless of how many times he had done it.

'Where did you find him?' asked Janice.

'In one of the warehouses behind the new Tesco. Not far from we found his car. Are you sure you don't know what he was doing there, Claire?'

'I have no idea,' said Claire in a voice that was now so quiet that the detectives could hardly hear it.

'And you're sure you didn't hear from him last night?'

'I told you I didn't,' said Claire. She gave Blizzard a sharp look. 'Why would you ask again? Don't you believe me?'

'Of course I do,' he said hurriedly. 'I didn't mean to sound like I don't. It's just that Alan would appear to have had a second mobile phone and he had a conversation with someone on it at about eight o'clock last night. We're trying to find out who it was. Did you know that he had a second phone?'

Claire shook her head.

'He never mentioned it,' she said. An edge pervaded her voice as she said, 'Maybe he was talking to that woman from the television company. Did you talk to her, like I suggested?'

'I did, yes,' said Blizzard. 'But I'm pretty sure that there's nothing between them.'

'You say that,' began Claire. 'But–'

'Come on, Claire,' said Janice. 'You're just tormenting yourself. Listen to Mr Blizzard. There's no way that Alan was having an affair.'

Silence settled on the room for a few moments. It was broken by Janice.

'Do you have any idea who might have killed him?' she asked.

'Not at this stage,' said Blizzard. 'We should know more after the post-mortem this afternoon. At least we'll know what kind of gun was used.'

Claire burst into tears.

## Chapter nine

The briefing room at Abbey Road Police Station was packed with journalists who had crammed in for the press conference, each one of them eager to hear the latest news about the death of Alan Steele. The murder of a police officer was a sensational story and every scrap of information was seized on with gusto. Excited conversation rippled round the gathering as a solemn Ronald and Blizzard took their seats behind the desk at the front of the room.

The chief inspector's presence added extra spice to the event and Ronald tried not to look worried but, as ever when it came to encounters between Blizzard and the media, it proved difficult. The inspector's poor relationship with journalists had often spilled over into rancour over the years. It was not that he did not recognise the valuable role that news outlets performed, particularly in inquiries where assistance from the public was important, but rather that he objected to what he regarded as the sensationalistic approach from some of the journalists. Blizzard and Ronald both knew that there were some reporters, mainly those writing for the national tabloids, who deliberately sought opportunities to evoke a reaction from the inspector by asking questions which he regarded as intrusive and which held the promise of an angry response. It was a tactic which had brought them plenty of headlines down the years.

Ronald, on the other hand, was a more skilled operator whose diplomatic skills came to the fore when he dealt with the media and now the room fell silent as he stood up. As he did so, Blizzard noticed that Sally Jackson was sitting at the back of the room, next to one of the company's cameramen, who was filming proceedings. Noting the inspector looking at her, Jackson gave a slight smile. Blizzard did not respond and returned his attention to Arthur Ronald.

'Thank you for your attendance, ladies and gentlemen,' said the superintendent. 'You will all have seen the press release, I imagine, but if you haven't, I can confirm that Detective Sergeant Alan Steele's body was found in a warehouse down by the river this morning, fifteen hours after he went missing yesterday evening. He had been shot and I can confirm that we are treating his death as murder.'

A low murmur ran round the room. Ronald waited for it to die away before continuing.

'As you can imagine,' he continued when the room was silent once more, 'this has come as a terrible shock to his friends and family and I would appeal to you to respect their privacy. His death has also shocked his colleagues within the police service. Alan was a much-valued and popular member of Western Division CID. This was a callous and cruel act and we will leave no stone unturned in our efforts to track down his killer.'

Having delivered the obligatory sound bites, Ronald looked round the room.

'Does anyone have any questions for myself or DCI Blizzard, who is leading the inquiry?' he asked.

'Do you have anyone in custody or any suspects?' asked a radio reporter.

'We are following up a number of leads,' said Ronald blandly.

'What kind of leads?'

'I can't give you any more details.'

'We heard that you raided a house in Tennyson Avenue in the early hours of this morning,' said another reporter. 'Can we assume that it was connected with the murder of DS Steele?'

'I would not like to comment at this stage,' said Ronald. 'As I am sure you can appreciate, the inquiry is in its early stages. Any more questions?'

'I have one for DCI Blizzard,' said a man in the front row.

Blizzard gave him a bleak look; both he and Ronald recognised the man as a Hafton-based freelance reporter who specialised in supplying the tabloids with sensationalist stories.

'What do you want to know?' asked Blizzard.

'Do you think that Detective Sergeant Steele's growing profile as a television personality had anything to do with his death?' The journalist gave the inspector a sly look. 'He's all over the trailers that have been running for the new series. I mean, he must have been the best-known detective in Hafton, mustn't he? Do you think that someone within the criminal fraternity might have objected to some of the things he has been saying? He's been quite outspoken, hasn't he?'

Before replying, Blizzard glanced at Sally Jackson, who was sitting forward, waiting intently for the inspector's answer.

'Any link with the television programme would be pure speculation,' he said. 'And you should know by now that I don't indulge in speculation.'

Jackson gave a nod of approval and sat back in her seat.

'Yes, but it is true that you have been uncomfortable with some of his activities, isn't it?' persisted the reporter.

'Was that because you were aware of the risks associated with him having a higher profile?'

'Who told you that I disapproved?' said Blizzard sharply. He wondered, as always in such situations, about the source of the journalists' information; the last thing he needed was someone leaking stories to the media on what was already a sensitive inquiry.

'Everyone knows that you do not like all the cameras being around,' said the reporter. 'Do you think Sergeant Steele would still be alive if it wasn't for the television series?'

Blizzard glanced at Sally Jackson; the producer was looking worried again.

'No comment,' he said.

'Yes, but–'

'Can we move on, please?' said Ronald. 'Suffice to say that, as it stands, there is nothing to suggest a connection between Alan's death and the television series.'

To the detectives' relief, the moment passed and after a few more questions, Ronald brought proceedings to a close with an appeal for information from the public. The press conference broke up and the journalists streamed from the room. Sally Jackson was among the last to leave and stopped on her way out.

'Thank you, Chief Inspector,' she said. 'We have already received several calls from journalists asking the same question. The crew were very fond of Alan and to have it suggested that we might be responsible in some way for his death is very upsetting for them.'

'I'm sure it is,' said Blizzard. He glanced round to make sure that no one could overhear their conversation. 'Can we make time for a chat later today? Alan mentioned that he might be working on some documentaries but wouldn't tell us what they were about and we really do need to know.'

'I won't be able to tell you much because the details are confidential.'

'Nothing is confidential in a murder inquiry,' said Blizzard.

'And like I said–'

'Say 3pm in my office?'

For a few moments Jackson looked like she was about to object but she thought better of it, nodded and left the room. Blizzard glanced at Ronald.

'She's hiding something,' said the inspector as he watched her go. 'I'm sure of it.'

'Do you think it's possible that Alan got himself on the wrong side of someone who did not wish to feature in one of the documentaries?' asked the superintendent.

'It's got to be a possibility.'

A young woman, who looked like she was aged little more than eighteen, had been waiting for Blizzard to finish his conversation with Sally Jackson and now she approached the inspector.

'Can I have a word?' she asked respectfully.

'And you are?' asked Blizzard.

The teenager presented the inspector with her business card, which identified her as Jenny Morton, a reporter for *The West Hafton Community News.*

'I'm sorry, I'm not sure that I have heard of it,' said the inspector. He passed it to Ronald, who shook his head.

'Me neither,' he said.

'We only set up a few weeks ago,' said Morton. 'We're a citizen newspaper. Local news for local people. We're delivered to eight hundred homes by volunteers.'

Ronald returned the card to Blizzard, who slipped it into his jacket pocket. Something about her youth and eager expression struck a chord with him and he did not seek to dismiss her in his usual cursory manner, as he would have done with some of the more experienced reporters.

'How can I help you?' he asked.

'I didn't want to mention anything in the press conference,' said Morton. 'I didn't want to give away my exclusive.'

'What exclusive?'

'I spent an hour with Alan Steele last week,' said Morton. 'We went for a coffee.'

'Why did you see him?' asked Blizzard suspiciously; he frowned on his officers talking to the media without approval.

'I wanted him to write a weekly column for us. Anyway, that's when he mentioned that he was working on something big.'

'Did he say what it was?' asked the inspector.

'He wouldn't give me any details,' said Morton. 'He said that it was the biggest thing to happen to him in his career but when I tried to find out more, he clammed up. I got the impression that he wished he had not said anything. Do you know what it was?'

Blizzard glanced at Ronald, who shrugged.

'I understand that you might not want to give me many details,' said Morton. Her voice was a little more forceful now. 'But, surely, you can tell me something?'

She took her notebook out of her jacket pocket.

'Perhaps you could give me some kind of a quote for the article?' she said. 'Even if it is just to confirm that he was working on a major inquiry?'

'But I don't know that he was,' replied Blizzard. 'I genuinely have no idea what he was talking about.'

Morton looked disappointed.

'It was going to be my first big exclusive,' she said.

'Sorry,' said Blizzard.

Morton left the room, watched by a thoughtful Blizzard. Marie Lindsay, one of the force's press officers, walked across to the detectives.

'What was that about?' she asked.

'She says that Alan told her he was working on something big,' said Blizzard.

'And was he?'

'Not that we know,' said Blizzard. He took the card out of his pocket. 'What do you know about *The West Hafton Community News*?'

'It's all grassroots stuff,' said the press officer. 'Knitting circles, line-dancing clubs, that sort of thing. Hardly the type of publication to get hold of a big crime exclusive.'

'Yet Alan mentioned something to her,' said Blizzard. 'Everything we learn about the man suggests that he had plenty of secrets – and that makes me nervous.'

# Chapter ten

Blizzard met Colley in the car park behind Abbey Road Police Station shortly before 1pm and drove them the short distance to the general hospital, where they had arranged to meet Home Office pathologist Peter Reynolds in the mortuary for Alan Steele's post-mortem.

'Reynolds had better not try it on today,' said Blizzard as he brought the car to a halt in the hospital car park. His head was beginning to throb as the lack of sleep began to catch up with him. 'I really am not in the mood for his games.'

'Are you ever?' said Colley.

Blizzard grunted something unintelligible as he got out of the car and Colley chuckled. The sergeant, like all the officers at Abbey Road, was aware of the fractious relationship which had developed between Blizzard and Reynolds over the years. A few minutes later, he was leaning against the wall in the mortuary watching as the latest encounter between the two men got under way.

Reynolds busied himself around the body, crouched over the table and humming quietly beneath his breath. Occasionally, the pathologist glanced at the inspector and gave knowing smiles. A balding middle-aged man with piggy eyes gleaming out of a chubby face, Reynolds knew that Blizzard had never liked him and played up to the situation whenever the opportunity arose. Colley would normally have relished the prospect of another meeting between the two – his colleagues always demanded word by word accounts afterwards – but this time was different. This time, the body on the slab was one of their own. This time, they were playing to different rules.

Blizzard watched with growing irritation as the pathologist continued to examine the body slowly and thoroughly.

'Can't you go any faster?' asked the detective. 'I've got a lot to do.'

'Patience, my dear Chief Inspector,' said the pathologist. He did not look up from the body. 'These things cannot be hurried.'

'But surely the cause of death is straightforward?' said Blizzard. 'I mean, there's a bloody big bullet hole in his head, isn't there?'

'One should never assume anything in this line of work,' said Reynolds. He gave Blizzard a sly look then glanced at Colley and winked. 'Surely, you've learned that by now?'

Blizzard glowered at him but said nothing. Despite the gravity of the situation, Colley smiled slightly and filed the line away; dead colleague or not, it would play well when he recounted the conversation to fellow officers later. The room was silent for a few minutes as the pathologist continued his examination, still humming under his breath as he leaned over the detective's body. As usual with Reynolds' post-mortems, Colley found himself fascinated by the deft way that the pathologist's long fingers moved across the body. The sergeant looked away as Reynolds prised open the skull. Eventually, Reynolds gave a slight exclamation of satisfaction and held up a bullet that was gripped in his tweezers.

'Definitely some kind of handgun,' he said. The pathologist gave an exclamation of surprise as he leaned forward to peer closer. He reached into a drawer, from which he produced a magnifying glass and continued his perusal of the bullet. 'Well, well, well.'

'Something interesting?' asked Blizzard.

The pathologist did not reply but instead walked across to the microscope on a nearby bench, where he examined the bullet further before straightening up.

'Well, what is it?' asked Blizzard irritably.

'Suffice to say that your investigation has taken a somewhat unexpected turn,' replied Reynolds. 'The gun that fired this bullet was a Beretta and should really be in the Crime Museum. And it's not the first time I have seen a bullet that was fired from it.'

'It isn't?' said Colley in surprise.

'It isn't,' said Reynolds. He was enjoying the impact that his words were having and stood back and gestured to the microscope. 'Take a look for yourself.'

It was Blizzard, his irritation replaced by curiosity, who accepted the opportunity first, placing his eye down to the viewer. He was silent for a few moments then straightened up and looked at the pathologist in disbelief.

'Is that what I think it is?' he said.

'It certainly is,' said Reynolds. There was a gleam in his eye. 'I told you things had taken a dramatic turn.'

'Is someone going to tell me what's happening?' asked Colley.

The pathologist gestured for the sergeant to take a look down the scope.

'You will see that someone has etched the letters *A S* into the bullet,' he said.

'I see that,' said Colley. He peered into the scope for a few more seconds then looked at the pathologist. 'For Alan Steele, one must assume.'

'One must indeed,' replied Reynolds. 'It's his trademark, after all.'

'Whose trademark?' asked the sergeant.

'No one knows,' said Reynolds. 'But every time the gun has been used, the initials of the victim have been etched into the bullet before it is placed in the weapon. Literally, your name on the bullet that killed you. A hitman with a certain elan, you might say.'

'But one who is as ruthless as they come,' said Blizzard grimly. 'It's become known as the Murder Gun, David, and it's been linked to at least five murders that I know of.'

The inspector glanced at Reynolds.

'However,' he said, 'I think I'm right in saying that there's been no record of it being used for at least ten years. Maybe fifteen?'

'That would be about right,' said the pathologist. 'It's certainly been out of circulation for a long time.'

'How come you know about it?' Colley asked.

'Because the first shooting was in our area,' said the pathologist. 'Over on the east side. Long before you joined the force. In fact, it was one of the first post-mortems I carried out.'

Colley looked at Blizzard.

'And you know about it because you were involved with the case, were you?' he asked.

'Only on the periphery,' said the inspector. 'I hadn't been that long in CID.'

'Who was the victim?' asked Colley.

'A gang leader called Mad Willy,' said Blizzard. He furrowed his brow for a moment or two as he tried to remember the dead man's full name. 'Willy Jacobs, as I recall.'

Reynolds nodded.

'He was a right headcase,' continued Blizzard. 'He ran a protection racket over on the east side. Liked to attack people with a claw hammer.'

'Oddly enough,' said Reynolds, glancing down at the body of Alan Steele, 'his body was found near the warehouse where your colleague was discovered. A coincidence, is it not?'

'Maybe it's not a coincidence,' said Blizzard. 'Maybe someone is sending us a message. Although God knows what it means.'

'Was anyone arrested for Mad Willy's murder?' said Colley.

'No one was arrested for any of them,' said Blizzard. 'It was always assumed that the killer was a professional hitman who left the area immediately after he committed the murder.'

'He hasn't come to the best bit yet,' said Reynolds with a slight smile. 'You see, there was a suspect for the man who hired him.'

'Who was it?' asked the sergeant. He noted the troubled expression on Blizzard's face. 'Or don't I want to know?'

Blizzard delayed his reply for dramatic effect.

'Nathaniel Callaghan,' he said eventually.

Colley stared at him.

'*The* Nathaniel Callaghan?' he said.

'God forbid that there ever be two of them,' said Blizzard. 'The theory was that Mad Willy had been trying to muscle in on Callaghan's territory and that he was killed as a warning to anyone else thinking of trying the same thing. Whatever the reason, it worked. It didn't take Callaghan long after Mad Willy's murder to become top dog.'

'But he was never charged?' asked the sergeant.

'You know him,' said the inspector. 'Careful as they come. There's detectives who have devoted their entire careers to getting him into a courtroom and failed.'

Colley looked down at the body and frowned.

'This has just got a whole lot more complicated,' he said.

'It certainly has,' said Blizzard. 'And the big question is what the hell was Alan doing dealing with a man like Callaghan, who has not been active in Hafton for the best part of twenty years? What's more, they were simply not in the same league. I can't think of any reason why their paths would cross.'

'And if they did, and Alan was getting in that deep, why didn't he tell anyone?' said Colley.

'Questions, questions,' replied Blizzard. He started walking towards the door. 'Like I keep saying, our Sergeant Steele turns out to be a man of many secrets and I don't like the sound of any of them.'

The inspector pushed open the door and disappeared into the corridor.

'No, don't thank me,' said Reynolds as Blizzard disappeared into the corridor. 'I'm just happy to help.'

Colley gave the pathologist an apologetic shrug.

'Sorry,' he said.

'I keep telling you that there's no need to apologise for your boss,' said Reynolds. He gave a smile. 'I am afraid that our encounter has given you very little with which to entertain your colleagues.'

'The line about never assuming anything was a nice one,' said the sergeant, also heading for the door.

'It was but I've given you rather thin pickings. However, on this occasion, I am prepared to make an exception. I don't blame your boss for being distracted. The last thing we want is a rerun of the last time Nathaniel Callaghan was in the city.'

# Chapter eleven

'The Angel of Death is right,' said Graham Ross as he walked into Blizzard's office later that afternoon. The division's forensics chief sat down and dropped a brown file onto the inspector's desk. 'It *is* the Murder Gun.'

'Definitely?' said the inspector.

'I am afraid so.' Ross withdrew a piece of paper from the file. 'You were almost right about the number of murders in which it has been used. There have been six others, not five. All of the victims were killed by a single shot to the head and the bullets were signed with their initials.'

Ross glanced down at the piece of paper.

'Mad Willy was the first time it was used,' he said. 'Shot in October 1997. His body was found behind one of the fruit importer's warehouses down by the river.'

'Sounds horribly familiar,' said Blizzard. 'Where were the other killings?'

'Leeds. They happened after Callaghan switched his operations away from Hafton.' Ross referred once more to the piece of paper. 'The second one was a small-time villain called Sammy Hales two years after Willy Jacobs was murdered. His body was found under a road bridge.'

Ross ran his finger down the piece of paper.

'The other shootings were fairly evenly spaced out,' he said. 'The last one was in 2012.'

'And the only thing that links the victims is the Murder Gun?'

'That and the fact that the victims had all crossed Nathaniel Callaghan in some way,' said Ross. 'There's a pattern. Each victim was a more significant villain than the previous one. The last murder, David Maskell in 2012, was of the leader of the only crime family in Leeds that could realistically challenge Callaghan. Clearly, Nathaniel was assassinating his way to the top.'

'Makes sense.'

'Yes, but Alan's death doesn't fit the pattern, does it?' said Ross. 'The Murder Gun hasn't been used for more than ten years, Callaghan has not had any interest in Hafton for even longer and Alan has never had any dealings with him, as far as we know.'

'As far as we know,' said Blizzard. 'Maybe he *did* have a connection with Callaghan and it's just that we haven't found out what it was yet.'

'But what kind of conn…?' began Ross. He did not finish the sentence and looked at the inspector in dismay as realisation dawned. 'Hang on, you're not suggesting that he was bent, are you? Because if you are…'

'What if I was?' said Blizzard. 'Haven't I always said that no question is off limits in a murder investigation, however unpalatable the answer might turn out to be? We follow where the evidence takes us.'

'I know, but *Alan*?'

'No one is beyond suspicion, Versace. As it goes, I am not suggesting that he was corrupt. However, I *am* wondering if the television company has been foolish enough to try to make a documentary about Callaghan and Alan was part of it.'

'Foolish would be the word,' said Ross. 'I mean, he's not exactly media-friendly, is our Nathaniel. And it would explain why Alan was so secretive about it.'

'It would indeed,' said Blizzard. He stood up. 'Right, I want everyone in the briefing room in half an hour.'

* * *

Thirty minutes later, the inspector was standing in front of his officers again. The briefing room's noticeboard, which had been covered up during the press conference to conceal its contents from the prying eyes of curious journalists, was once more on show. The photographs of the four teenage drug dealers had been removed and in their place was an image taken outside a church, showing a gathering of people of all ages, at the front of which, his face circled in black ink, was a thin man with wispy white hair, a goatee beard and piercing blue eyes. He was wearing an expensive grey suit with a white carnation in the buttonhole and below the image was the handwritten caption *Nathaniel Callaghan.*

Detectives young and old stared at the image in silent fascination; even the youngest among the gathering had heard the name. Nathaniel Callaghan's status in the highest echelons of organised crime meant that he merited the overused description 'legend'. He was, some people said, a true 'untouchable' and there had been rumours for many years that more than one senior police officer was on his payroll. Not that anyone used the word 'untouchable' in the presence of John Blizzard or Arthur Ronald, who was sitting at the back of the room. Both men had made it clear from the moment they had taken over their roles that no one was beyond the law. The selection of Hafton gangland figures who were now languishing in jail stood testament to the fact.

Blizzard tapped the picture.

'To put an end to any speculation,' he said, 'yes, the gun that killed Alan has links to Nathaniel Callaghan and yes, he is our number one suspect.'

A murmur ran round the room. Blizzard waited for silence to return before continuing.

'I have called this briefing,' he said, 'because it is important that you know exactly what kind of a man we are dealing with. In case you are wondering, this picture was taken six months ago at a family wedding in Leeds. Nathaniel is under pretty much constant surveillance and the picture was taken by West Yorkshire Police's Organised Crime Unit. Not that Nathaniel would ever be as careless as to be caught committing a crime on camera. He likes to play the law-abiding citizen. It appeals to his sense of humour. He's even joined the Rotary Club and he has not even picked up so much as a parking ticket in the thick end of fifty years.'

Blizzard turned to focus his attention on the younger officers in the room.

'Some of you may be tempted to regard him as yesterday's man because of his advanced age,' he said. The inspector gave a slight smile as he looked at the younger officers in the room. 'I know the feeling.'

The comment was met with smiles.

'But don't be misled by the fact that Nathaniel is in his seventies,' continued Blizzard. 'He's as dangerous now as ever he was. What happened to Alan should be sufficient to convince you of that.'

The inspector paused to ensure that the switch from humour to deadly serious had had the desired effect. The solemn expression on the detectives' faces suggested that it had.

'A little biography,' he continued. 'Callaghan was born in Hafton and started his criminal career here in the late sixties. His gang were into just about anything you could think of, protection rackets, smuggling, extortion, blackmail, stealing stuff from Hafton Docks. When

Hafton became too small for his ambitions, he moved to Leeds. Although he is still based there, he does not engage in activities in the city and instead switched his focus to trafficking firearms on a global scale a long time ago.'

'But, famously, not trafficking drugs,' said Chris Ramsey.

'But famously not drugs, no,' said Blizzard. 'He has never been involved in drugs or allowed any of his gang to deal in them. He regards them as evil.'

'And guns aren't?' said Sarah Allatt, who was sitting in the front row.

'Feel free to argue the point with him, if you fancy, Sarah,' said Blizzard. 'I'll hold your coat while you debate the philosophy behind his crimes.'

Laughter rippled round the room.

'Er, no thanks,' said Allatt quickly. 'He doesn't sound very pleasant company.'

'Au contraire,' said Blizzard. He glanced at Colley, who was leaning against the wall as usual. 'He can be charming, can't he, David?'

'In a terrifying kind of way,' said the sergeant. He shuddered at the memory. 'There's nothing more frightening than a polite gangster.'

'You went to see him over something to do with his grandson last year, didn't you?' asked Allatt.

Blizzard nodded.

'The boy was stupid enough to get himself arrested over here on a drug dealing charge,' he said. 'Nathaniel asked us to go to Leeds to see him. He was politeness personified but when he thought that things were not going his way a day or so later, he showed the other side of his personality. All menace and threats. It was an example of the many contradictions which make up his personality.'

'What happened to his grandson?' asked Allatt.

'The CPS charged him but a few weeks later, the case was mysteriously dropped. Nathaniel may be long gone from the city but, clearly, he still has influence.'

The inspector looked at Arthur Ronald, who was sitting at the back of the room.

'We never really got to the bottom if it, did we?' he said.

The superintendent shook his head.

'Not really,' he said. 'Clearly, he whispered in someone's ear. We never found out who.'

'I heard that Callaghan is a very religious man,' said Jenny Carr. 'Is that true?'

'It is, yes,' said Blizzard. 'His parents were devout Christians and brought him up to be the same. He still regularly attends church and insisted that both his boys went to Sunday school. However, he may praise the Lord on a Sunday but the rest of the week is strictly reserved for a celebration the ways of Mammon. He'll ship crates of guns to any passing loony.'

'How did he get into arms dealing?' asked Allatt.

'He supplied some firearms to the IRA in the eighties and it went from there,' said Blizzard. 'Now, half the rogue governments in the world get their guns from him, as do plenty of extremists, everyone from Chechen separatists to Islamic State fighters, and half the crazy terrorist groups in Africa. Oh, and the Russian and Italian mafias.'

The inspector turned back to the noticeboard.

'So that's Nathaniel Callaghan,' he said thoughtfully. 'Underestimate him at your peril, ladies and gentlemen. Everyone from UK anti-terrorist units and the National Crime Agency to Interpol and the FBI have been after him for years but he'll do whatever is required to protect himself.'

'So how come he was interested in Alan?' asked Jenny Carr. The constable looked round at the others. 'Surely, he wasn't a threat to him. I mean I've never heard him mention Callaghan. Has anyone else?'

There were the shakes of heads all round.

'We've been going through everything that Alan has been doing since Javelin launched,' said Chris Ramsey. 'But there's nothing to explain why a high-roller like Callaghan would be interested in him and I don't think that he was bent. He was honest as the day was long, was Alan.'

The comment was greeted with nods of agreement. Blizzard said nothing but noticed that Graham Ross had glanced at him when the comment was made. Blizzard returned his attention to Chris Ramsey.

'Did you get chance to take a look at Alan's career record?' he asked. 'He was based in South Yorkshire before he came here, I think.'

'For three years,' said Ramsey. He glanced down at a document on his lap. 'He joined after leaving sixth form college and served as a uniformed officer in his hometown of Rotherham before transferring over here in 2004 to become a detective constable. There's nothing on his record to raise any flags.'

'OK,' said Blizzard. 'So, Nathaniel Callaghan has to be the main focus of our inquiry and we carry on looking for the connection but keep things low-profile, the fewer people who know that we are investigating Callaghan the better. Like I said, he has a lot of influential friends. Do I make myself clear?'

There were nods all round then the room fell silent for a few moments. Blizzard knew what the officers were all thinking. It was what everyone had been thinking from the moment the body had been found. Sarah Allatt was the one to give it a voice.

'Do you think any of us are in danger?' she asked.

'I wish I could say no,' said Blizzard. 'But I can't, so watch your backs and be careful what you say and who you say it to. Trust no one.'

## Chapter twelve

'You've really got it in for us, haven't you?' said Sally Jackson. She gave Blizzard an angry look across his desk. The briefing had just finished and she had made her way to his office for their 3pm meeting as agreed. 'First of all, you try to make out that I have been having an affair with Alan and then you suggest that he might have been killed because of something that he was working on for us. This is starting to feel like victimisation.'

'It's nothing of the sort,' said Blizzard. 'But whatever Alan was involved in, it got him killed and I need to know why. I would have thought you would have welcomed that. After all, you and your people could also be at risk.'

The producer's confrontational demeanour was replaced by something more vulnerable.

'Do you really think we are in danger?' she asked.

'I have no idea. However, until we find out what's been happening, it's got to be a possibility.'

'Do you think the murder was organised by the drug dealer who threatened Alan?'

'We think it's unlikely,' said Blizzard.

'Then who?' asked the producer.

'Like I said, we are interested in the documentaries that Alan mentioned yesterday afternoon. I really do need to know what they are about.'

'I can't say.'

'Can't or won't?'

'Both,' said Jackson. Jackson's vulnerability had been replaced by something more guarded as her professional persona re-emerged. 'What you have to understand is that the television industry is very competitive and that details of new projects are zealously protected in case someone else steals the idea.'

'Might I remind you that this is a murder inquiry?'

'You don't need to remind me of that,' said Jackson sharply. Her eyes flashed defiance. 'You act like you're the only ones who have lost a friend. Well, you're not. My team are very upset that Alan is dead. And before you say it, not just because we're going to have to find another presenter.'

The comment seemed genuine enough so Blizzard softened his approach.

'I appreciate that,' he said. 'And I apologise. That was insensitive of me. Are you sure you can't tell me anything?'

'Only that I can't see any of our projects being important enough to drive someone to kill him. There's loads of similar films on Netflix and other channels and, as far as I know, no one has ever been murdered for appearing in something like that.'

'Wasn't Jill Dando murdered at the time she was presenting *Crimewatch*?' said Blizzard. 'What if someone took against Alan in the same way? A gangland figure, for instance?'

'What makes you say that?' asked Jackson sharply. 'Have you heard something?'

'It's just a thought.'

'Well, you can rest assured that we are not dealing with anyone like that,' said the producer. She glanced at the clock on the wall and stood up. 'I have to go. I'm sorry I could not be more helpful.'

'I could charge you with obstruction,' said Blizzard. 'Force you to be more helpful.'

Jackson looked at him with a slight smile on her face.

'I wonder what Superintendent Ronald would say to that?' she said.

'What's it got to do with him?'

'I am off to interview him for an episode of the programme devoted to Alan's memory,' said Jackson. 'He wishes to say a few words in tribute. I don't think he'd be impressed if you arrested me, do you?'

Blizzard gave her a rueful look and wafted a hand towards the door.

'Go on,' he said.

After she had departed, the inspector sat for a few moments, suddenly aware of how tired he felt. With his eyes growing heavy, he had just started to make a cup of tea to revive himself when there was a knock on the office door and one of the reception staff walked in.

'I'm sorry to interrupt, sir,' she said, 'but there are a couple of officers to see you from the National Crime Agency in London. One of them says she knows you from her days at West Yorkshire.'

'Sounds like Wendy Talbot,' said Blizzard.

'That's her.'

'Show them in, will you?'

The kettle had just boiled when Blizzard turned round with the box of teabags in his hand to see a middle-aged woman with short brown hair enter the office, accompanied by a lean man in his thirties. The woman was smiling.

'See,' said Wendy Talbot, glancing at her colleague, 'I told you that he lives on cups of tea.'

Blizzard returned the smile. He and Talbot had worked together on several joint operations involving their respective forces, and targeted at organised crime, and the inspector had come to value her sound judgement and no-nonsense approach to the job. They mirrored his own.

'Wendy,' he said. He put the box of teabags down and shook her hand. 'Good to see you again.'

'I just wish it could have been in happier circumstances, John. I'm sorry about your guy.' Talbot gestured to her colleague. 'This is Matt Riley. He's a DS with West Yorkshire but he's been on secondment to the NCA for two months.'

'Welcome to Hafton, Sergeant,' said Blizzard. He shook the sergeant's hand as well.

'Actually, I've been here quite a few times to play rugby against your force's team,' said Riley. 'David Colley works with you, I think?'

'He does,' said Blizzard. He gestured for his guests to take a seat at the desk. 'Are you responsible for the black eyes he keeps coming in with on a Monday morning?'

'Some of them, I suspect,' said Riley. He rolled up his right trouser leg to reveal a scar on his knee. 'And he's responsible for some of my injuries.'

Blizzard raised his eyes to the ceiling in mock disapproval. His attention turned to the kettle and after they were all seated with mugs of tea in hand, he looked at Talbot.

'Do I assume that you're here because you heard about the Murder Gun and Alan's link with Nathaniel Callaghan?' he asked.

'We already knew about their connection.'

'You did?' Blizzard looked at her suspiciously. 'How come?

'I know that this is a difficult time for you, but I'm afraid that I'm going to make it worse,' said Talbot. She gave him an apologetic look. 'You see, Alan featured in one of NCA's surveillance operations.'

Blizzard's eyes narrowed.

'You had one of my officers under surveillance and didn't think to tell me?' he said. 'That's out of order, Wendy.'

'Keep your hair on. It wasn't like that. We were watching someone else when your guy turned up out of the blue. We were as surprised as you are and we were going to come and see you anyway. Then we heard that your ballistics people were asking questions about the Murder Gun and it became more urgent.' Talbot nodded at Riley. 'Show him, Matt.'

Riley opened his briefcase and produced a photograph, which he slid across the desk to Blizzard. It showed a swarthy, shaven-headed man, aged in his late forties and wearing a dark suit. He was talking to Alan Steele in what appeared to be a deserted multistorey car park at night.

'This was taken several days ago in Leeds,' said Riley. 'The other guy's our target but one of our people recognised Alan Steele from the television.'

'And who *is* the other guy?' asked Blizzard. 'He looks foreign?'

'That's Ray Varone,' said Riley. He gave a slight smile. 'Part-Italian, part-Pudsey. His father was a member of the Mafia in Milan and his mother worked in a florist in Pudsey. Think Don Corleone talking like Eddie Waring. Apparently, he likes pizza *and* Yorkshire puddings.'

Blizzard chuckled; despite the gravity of the situation, there was something about Matt Riley that he liked, something that he also saw in David Colley, an ability to mix professionalism with much-needed humour. The inspector peered closer at the picture.

'So *that's* Ray Varone, is it?' he said. 'I'm not sure I've ever seen a picture of him.'

'I'm not surprised,' said Talbot. 'He keeps a very low profile.'

'Why have you been watching him?' asked Blizzard.

'Because he is Callaghan's right-hand man and anything he does is interesting. He's the one who will take over from the old man when he eventually decides to retire.'

'Really?' said Blizzard. 'I thought it would be his two sons.'

'According to our information, Callaghan has never fully trusted them and he's getting more paranoid the older he gets. However, he trusts Varone implicitly.'

'Presumably that hasn't gone down well with his sons,' said Blizzard.

'Not sure they're in a position to object,' said Riley. 'Neither of them are in good health.'

'Is the change imminent?' asked Blizzard. 'Is Nathaniel planning to step aside?'

'We don't think so,' said Talbot. 'But he is seventy-two and he can't go on for ever. The main reason we have been watching Varone, though, is that we received a tip-off that Callaghan has been approached to sell firearms to a Moroccan crime syndicate that wants to muscle in on drug territories in London, Birmingham and Manchester. They need to increase their firepower and as everyone knows, if you want to increase your firepower, you shop at Callaghan's. Varone is acting as the middle-man on the deal. I don't need to tell you how ugly it would be if it went through.'

'No indeed,' said Blizzard. He looked at the picture again and a tight knot formed in the pit of his stomach as he wondered if he was looking at the man who had ordered the murder of his detective sergeant. 'So, where does Alan fit into things? Surely all this is well above his league?'

'We were hoping you could tell us,' said Talbot. She nodded at Riley, who produced another photograph from his briefcase and placed it on the desk next to the first image. 'See, he wasn't alone when he met Varone. There was a woman with him. Trouble is, we don't know who she is. She's not a police officer, as far as we can tell. We thought you might be able to put a name to the face.'

Blizzard stared down at the picture and gave a slight smile.

'Do you recognise her?' asked Talbot.

'Her name is Sally Jackson and she's just lied her head off to me.'

'I find that it's never a good idea to lie to John Blizzard,' said Talbot. 'Who is she?'

'She's a producer with the company that makes the reality show here. There's been talk of Alan quitting his job to make true crime documentaries and, given that he was killed with the Murder Gun, we have been thinking that they might be planning one about Callaghan. Sally denied it but I don't believe her.'

'Is she not aware how dangerous it would be to try to make a film about Callaghan?' asked Talbot.

Blizzard thought of Alan Steele's corpse lying in the mortuary.

'If she wasn't before, she is now,' he said.

'Do you know where we can find her?'

'The film company has an office here,' said Blizzard. 'It's in the next corridor.'

'Then I think we should go and talk to her,' said Talbot.

'I think you're right,' said the inspector.

# Chapter thirteen

Sally Jackson and cameraman Bob Harrold were watching a playback of the interview that they had just filmed with Arthur Ronald when Blizzard and his visitors walked into their office unannounced.

'Haven't you heard of knocking?' protested the producer.

Blizzard ignored the question.

'These officers are from the National Crime Agency,' he said. 'They would like to speak to you.'

Talbot and Riley held up their identifications cards for her to read.

'What about?' asked Jackson. She made little effort to conceal her irritation at the interruption as she picked up the remote control and froze the image of Arthur Ronald on the screen. 'We really are rather busy.'

'As are we all,' said Blizzard. He gave the cameraman a look. 'It's rather a sensitive matter, and one that would be better discussed alone.'

'I have no secrets from my team,' said Jackson.

'Nevertheless, I think it would best if he left the room,' said Blizzard.

The cameraman looked as if he was about to say something but the stern expression on the faces of all three detectives made him think better of it. Sally Jackson had the same thought – the detectives didn't look in the mood to be obstructed in their work and she was acutely aware that tempers had shortened since the murder of Alan Steele. She shrugged.

'As you wish,' she said. She nodded at the cameraman. 'I'll be OK.'

'Give me a yell if you need me,' he said as he left the room, giving Blizzard a look. 'I'll just be outside.'

Once the cameraman had closed the door behind him, Jackson turned to the detectives.

'Why all the secrecy?' she said.

'Like I said,' replied Blizzard as the officers sat down, 'it's a delicate matter. About you and Alan.'

'Surely, you're not still going on about that daft rumour about us having an affair?' she said. 'You really don't give up, do you? I keep telling you, there is no "me and Alan". And even if there was anything between us, why on earth would the National Crime Agency be interested?'

'Because it's much more serious than an affair,' said Talbot. 'No, what interests us is the relationship between the two of you and Nathaniel Callaghan.'

If the detectives were expecting a dramatic reaction from the producer, they were to be disappointed. It seemed to all three officers that there was the briefest flicker of recognition on Jackson's face but it vanished in a second, to be replaced by an expression that was designed not to give anything away.

'I don't know what you're talking about,' said the producer. 'Who's Nathaniel Callaghan?'

'Don't take us for fools, Sally,' said Talbot. There was an edge to her voice now. 'You know exactly who he is.'

'OK, so maybe I've heard the name.'

'Presumably, you know that he's a major gangland figure then?' said Talbot.

'So what if he is? Why on earth would you think that me and Alan would have anything to do with him? I've never met the man. I don't even know what he looks like.'

'That may be true,' said Talbot. 'But what about Ray Varone? His right-hand man?'

'Never heard of him,' said Jackson dismissively. She looked at Blizzard. 'Don't you listen?'

'Perhaps you would like to explain this then,' said Talbot. She nodded to Riley, who placed the envelope containing the surveillance photographs on the desk. 'Because from where I am sitting, it makes you out to be a liar.'

Jackson looked uneasily at the envelope and Blizzard allowed himself the merest of smiles. It was one of the oldest tricks in the book; get someone to lie then present them with the evidence of their untruths. It never failed to unsettle people and it was a technique he'd used himself many times to great effect.

The producer, for her part, was acutely aware that her heart had started to race. She could feel beads of sweat glistening on her forehead as she watched with a mixture of fascination and dread as Riley removed the photograph from the envelope and placed it on the desk. Jackson stared at the image showing her with Steele and Varone in the car park. None of the detectives said anything, letting the heavy silence do its work.

'There's not much use in me denying that we've met him, is there?' said Jackson bleakly. 'Where did you get the picture?'

'Never mind that,' said Talbot. 'The more important question is why you and Detective Sergeant Steele were meeting a man like Ray Varone?'

Jackson did not reply.

'Come on, Sally,' said Blizzard. 'We'll find out eventually.'

Jackson thought for a few moments, gave a nod of resignation and emitted a heavy sigh. She knew when she was beaten. She looked at Blizzard.

'You must be loving this,' she said.

'Not with one of my officers lying on a slab in the mortuary, I'm not,' said Blizzard. 'Alan mentioned that he may be working on some documentaries. I take it that Nathaniel Callaghan was the subject of one of them?'

Jackson nodded.

'That was the plan,' she said. 'We want to make a two-part film for a series on the UK's biggest gangsters that has been commissioned by a new true crime channel called Murder Zone. They love the idea of gangsters with strong religious beliefs and want to call the series *The Real Godfathers*.'

'Very drole,' said Blizzard. 'You should have told me what was happening. I really did need to know that Alan was getting into something like that.'

'I couldn't. None of us could. The channel made us sign non-disclosure agreements. I shouldn't be talking to you, really.'

'Yes, well, I'd like to think that a murder inquiry trumps a non-disclosure agreement,' said the inspector. 'I take it that Alan was going to be part of the series?'

'He was going to front it,' said Jackson. 'It was going to be his big break. The people at Murder Zone love the idea of using former police officers as presenters. They say that it gives programmes more credibility and Alan was very good at it. He's a great loss.'

'How come you persuaded Ray Varone to talk to you?' asked Talbot. 'He's not exactly media-friendly.'

'Alan said that he had Ray's mobile number.'

'And how come?' asked Talbot. She glanced at Riley, who frowned. 'It's not as if Varone is in the phone book under V for Villain.'

'I don't know. Anyway, eventually he agreed to meet us. Varone told us that he'd have to talk to Callaghan.'

'I can't imagine that he would have been particularly enthusiastic about it,' said Talbot.

'You'd be surprised,' said Jackson. 'A lot of gang leaders like the media. They enjoy the notoriety. Look at the way the Kray twins behaved. And one of the executives at Murder Zone told me that they've got several gang leaders lined up for the new series. We hoped that might persuade Nathaniel to take part.'

'The fact that Alan is dead would seem to suggest that he had no intention of going along with it,' said Blizzard. 'You've been playing a very dangerous game, Sally.'

'I'm not stupid. I know what Callaghan is like. Besides, it might not have been him who ordered the killing. I'm sure that Alan made plenty of enemies during his career. You all have, I imagine.'

Blizzard nodded without realising that he done it; he'd faced down a number of his own enemies during his time as a police officer.

'Nevertheless, everything points to Nathaniel,' he said. 'But I can't go into detail. Suffice to say that you and your team really do need to be careful. If I were you, I'd drop the idea of making a film about him. It's way too risky.'

'I'll bear it in mind,' said Jackson.

But everyone in the room knew that she wouldn't. Five minutes later, with the conversation at an end, the three detectives were back in Blizzard's office.

'She's one tough cookie,' said Talbot. She frowned. 'And I'm puzzled by the fact that Alan had Varone's mobile number.'

'Me, too,' said Riley. 'Callaghan insists that everyone in his gang uses burner phones. Varone changes his every few days. Every time we think we have a number we can put a trace on, it's already out of date yet Alan Steele was able to ring him, no bother.'

'What are you suggesting?' said Blizzard, although he already knew the answer. 'That Alan might have been bent?'

'We certainly should not rule it out,' said Talbot. 'Sorry, John, I know it's the last thing you want to hear at a time like this but we have to ask the difficult questions. You know that.'

'I've been saying the same thing to my people,' said Blizzard. 'Are we assuming that Alan was shot to warn other people not to co-operate with the filmmakers then?'

'I'm not sure,' said Talbot. She frowned. 'There's still too many things that don't add up.'

'Such as?'

'Such as Callaghan has never ordered a hit on a police officer, as far as we know. He knows that if he pops a gangster, most cops will think that the victim deserved it anyway, but if he kills a cop, we'll not rest until the murderer has been locked up.'

'But we can't ignore the fact that Alan was killed by the Murder Gun,' said Blizzard.

'But why bring it out now, after all those years?' Talbot shook her head. 'And why use it when everyone knows it's connected to Callaghan?'

'To send out a message,' said Blizzard.

'Nathaniel Callaghan doesn't need to send out a message,' said Riley. 'Everyone knows that you don't mess with him. No, Wendy's right. There's something not right here. Too many questions to be answered.'

'Well, the only one person can answer them for us is Nathaniel Callaghan,' said Blizzard. 'We need to go and see him.'

There was a knock on the door and Colley walked in.

'Ah, David,' said Blizzard. 'I was just saying that we need to go and see Callaghan.'

'Yippy do,' said the sergeant without much in the way of enthusiasm.

'It's not that simple,' said Talbot. 'You know how political it gets around him, John. Everyone from MI5 to Interpol is watching him and the last thing they'll want is some detective from a small provincial force going in there and jeopardising larger inquiries. Sorry, John, I don't mean to be dismissive but you know the way these people think.'

'I do but, on the other hand, it'll look strange if we do not try to talk to him,' said Blizzard. 'He must know that once we identify the Murder Gun he'll be due a visit.'

'He's right,' said Riley.

'I guess so,' said Talbot. 'I'll make some calls, John. You'll need someone to watch your back, and you don't do politics so keep your nose out of it until I tell you you're good to go.'

'Sometimes,' said Blizzard, 'it can be difficult to work out who the good guys are.'

## Chapter fourteen

'Hafton was a wild place in those days,' said the grey-haired man as he sat down in an armchair and took a sip of tea. 'Particularly the east side. Much worse than it is today. But you'll know that anyway.'

Blizzard nodded. He was sitting in the living room of the bungalow owned by former uniformed inspector Charles Radley. Now in his eighties, Radley had long since retired but was the first person Blizzard thought of when he required information on the time Nathaniel Callaghan spent building his criminal empire in Hafton. Radley had been the first inspector to command the young Blizzard and Ronald and had guided the rookies through the early stages of their service on the east side before they made the move across the city to take up roles with CID at Abbey Road.

'I remember it well,' said Blizzard. He took a sip of tea and reached for a chocolate biscuit. Having dropped in on the pensioner on his way home, the inspector was feeling increasingly weary from lack of sleep and sensed that a sugar injection would help. 'My early days on the east side were a real eye-opener for a young lad from rural Lincolnshire.'

'I'll bet they were,' said Radley. He chuckled. 'The east side was a pretty lawless place and you and Arthur were like rabbits caught in the headlights in those early days. Mind, it didn't take you long to get over your nerves, as I recall.'

Radley took another sip of tea and looked intently at the former rookie.

'However,' he said, 'you are not here to reminisce about the bad old days with a wizened codger like me. Why so interested in Nathaniel Callaghan? Do I assume that it is something to do with the death of your detective?'

'What makes you say that?' asked Blizzard.

'What else could it be? In my experience, DCIs don't make social calls. But surely you don't believe that Nathaniel had anything to do with Sergeant Steele's murder? It's a long time since he had any interest in Hafton.'

'Between these four walls?' said Blizzard, and Radley nodded. 'It's looking very much like he ordered the killing.'

'That takes some believing,' said Radley. He took another sip of tea. 'Not least because I would not have said it was his style these days. I mean, he had Mad Willy Jacobs murdered, sure, and those guys in Leeds, but I got the impression that he moved on the more established he became. I think he saw it all as a bit beneath him. A bit vulgar. Is he still a God-botherer?'

'Very much so, although I do sometimes wonder if it's all an act.'

'No, it's genuine,' said Radley. 'His parents gave a whole new meaning to "devout".'

'You knew him pretty well, I think?'

'In his east side days, yes. I think he quite liked me. A lot of the officers kowtowed to him but I would have none of it. I think he found me a challenge. Something tells me you're the same.'

'I like to think so,' said Blizzard. 'What was he like in those days? I didn't really know him. I was only a rookie.'

'He was scary,' said Radley. 'He was unpredictable, that was the thing. You never knew what he was going to do next.'

'Was it common knowledge that he had Mad Willy Jacobs killed?'

'Oh, aye. Everyone knew it but CID could never prove it. You know what it's like with him – getting people to talk is nigh on impossible. Well, it was in those days and from what I hear nothing has changed.'

'Hear from who?' asked Blizzard.

'Oh, just some of the boys from the old days.'

'Do they know – do you know – who the shooter was?'

Radley gave him a shrewd look.

'So that's why you're here, is it?' he said. 'I did wonder. Was Alan Steele killed with the Murder Gun, by any chance?'

'He was. It was Reynolds that twigged when he found the bullet.'

'Is he still sanctimonious?' said Radley with a slight smile. 'I don't imagine he's changed.'

'He's just as bad as ever.'

'Do I take it your guy's initials were etched on the bullet that killed him?'

Blizzard nodded.

'Heavy stuff,' said Radley. 'And to answer your question, no, we never knew who the shooter was. We always assumed that it was someone who Callaghan brought in from the outside. But surely the gun hasn't been used for years?'

'No, it hasn't. That's why it's so puzzling that it should turn up now.'

'How come your guy had a connection with Callaghan?'

'That's the other puzzle,' said Blizzard. 'He didn't. Not that we know of, anyway.'

'Well there must be something,' said Radley.

'That's what worries me,' said Blizzard.

It worried the inspector on the drive home as well. Fee was sitting in the living room watching the television when he arrived.

'Where have you been?' she asked. 'I thought you were going to try to be home for nine. God knows what state the lasagna is in.'

'Sorry, love,' he said. He slumped into an armchair and closed his eyes as weariness overwhelmed him and his headache suddenly grew worse. 'I've been to see Charles Radley.'

'Why?'

Blizzard opened his eyes but did not reply.

'There's something you're not telling me,' said Fee. She fixed him with a hard stare. 'Come on, me-laddo, out with it. You know I won't tell anyone.'

'It's not that. I don't want to worry you.'

'It takes a lot to worry me,' said Fee.

'Well, this *is* a lot.'

'Come on, John,' she said. Her look was the look of a woman who would not be denied. 'I'm not like Claire Steele. Why did you see Charles?'

'I wanted to pick his brains about Nathaniel Callaghan.'

Fee's expression turned to one of uneasiness.

'Why?' she asked.

'It looks like he might be behind Alan's murder.'

Fee looked shocked.

'Are you sure?' she said. 'I mean, why would he harm someone like Alan? Surely, they move in different circles?'

'You'd think. And no, we're not a hundred per cent sure. Killing police officers is not really Nathaniel's style. Anyway, we're going to see him in the morning.'

'To arrest him?'

'We don't have enough evidence for that, not yet anyway, but we want to see what he has to say about it.'

Fee tried to look relaxed but Blizzard could sense that she was hiding acute anxiety. He knew what she was thinking and, eventually, she gave voice to it.

'Do you think that you might be in danger?' she asked quietly. 'Or any of the team?'

'People keep asking me that.'

'And what do you tell them?'

'That I don't know.'

# Chapter fifteen

The following morning, with Talbot and Riley heading back to London after staying overnight in Hafton, Blizzard and Colley made their way to Leeds where, as 10.30am approached, they found themselves sitting in the inspector's vehicle outside a nondescript two-storey office block on an industrial estate on the edge of the city. The sign across the front door read *N Callaghan and Sons Import and Export* and Blizzard gave a slight smile; Nathaniel Callaghan always did have a well-honed sense of irony.

The gangster had an even stronger sense of security, the inspector thought as he turned his attention to the raft of CCTV cameras that surveyed the car park and the approach road. They would have ensured that the officers' arrival on the industrial estate had not gone unnoticed. Blizzard knew they were being watched as they sat in the vehicle, as instructed, and waited for someone to come and get them.

The detectives were acutely aware that they were unwelcome visitors. That had been made clear in a terse telephone call the previous afternoon between Blizzard and a secretary whose clipped tones suggested a woman every bit as intimidating as her employer. Initially, she said that Callaghan had declined to meet them but persistence, and the threat of a high-profile arrest with the media present, had paid off and the secretary, who had been sounding increasingly irritated, eventually said that Callaghan had granted them ten minutes. They ought to be aware, she had added, that her boss was not pleased at the intrusion – and that ten minutes meant ten minutes.

Now, Blizzard sat in a state of eager anticipation; the inspector enjoyed jousting with people who thought that they were somehow superior to everyone else. Blizzard's mood was not mirrored in his colleague. David Colley had, during his career, faced down many a hardened villain and prided himself that he was not scared of anyone, but there was something different about Nathaniel Callaghan, not least the overwhelming sense that there was nothing of which the man was not capable. The death of his friend and fellow sergeant had done nothing to improve Colley's mood. Without realising he had done it, he shuddered slightly as he recalled their last meeting. Blizzard noticed and gave a slight smile.

'Just relax, will you?' he said. 'We'll be fine.'

'I imagine Alan thought the same thing,' said Colley.

Silence settled on the vehicle again. Eventually, a shaven-headed man in a dark suit emerged from the building and walked towards the car.

'That's Ray Varone,' said Blizzard.

Colley watched Varone with morbid interest; was he, he wondered, looking at the man who had murdered his friend? Varone beckoned for them to get out of the car and follow him into the building where he searched the detectives for concealed listening devices, then took them upstairs into an office where sat the secretary, all starched clothes, black-rimmed spectacles and attitude. She did not say anything when the detectives arrived but instead viewed them with undisguised disdain as she ushered them into the inner sanctum. On being shown into the spacious office, the detectives found Callaghan sitting behind his desk. The secretary finally spoke as she turned to return to her office.

'Ten minutes,' she said firmly, pointing at the wall clock. 'No more. Mr Callaghan is a very busy man.'

Callaghan gestured for them to sit down and gave them a slight smile.

'You mustn't mind Cynthia,' he said. 'She does like to look after me. She's a kind-hearted soul really. Anyway, welcome, Chief Inspector and the inestimable Sergeant Colley. I seem to recall that when last we met, your daughter had just started nursery. Laura must be at school now, I think?'

Colley was not worried at the comment. He knew that it was one of Callaghan's tried and trusted methods to unsettle police officers and had been expecting something similar. The comment was an easy one to make, thought the sergeant; it did not mean that Callaghan had actually instructed anyone to watch his daughter.

'She's just started,' he said with a knowing smile. 'Thank you for asking.'

Callaghan's next words wiped the smile off the sergeant's face.

'Grainger Street Primary, I think,' he said. 'The same school that your wife teaches at, I believe.'

'How the…?' began Colley, half-rising from his seat.

Blizzard reached out a hand and pushed him back then gave Callaghan a sharp look.

'Might I suggest that, if we've only got ten minutes, we don't waste time on your silly games?' he said.

'I was just making polite conversation,' said Callaghan.

The detectives could see from the angry glint in his eyes that he had not appreciated the inspector's comment; he was not used to being spoken to like that. The gangster had found over the years that the vast majority of police officers were wary of him, and tended to exhibit excessive respect, but the inspector did neither and that intrigued Callaghan, who had still not worked out whether to welcome the challenge or resent the lack of respect being exhibited. Not that his face betrayed any of these thoughts now. He tried to regain the initiative.

'I didn't have to see you, you know,' he said with an edge to his voice. 'One phone call and I could have made all this go away.'

'Then why didn't you?' asked Blizzard.

'Let's just call it curiosity, shall we?' he said. Callaghan gestured to the teapot and the three china cups and saucers on the desk.

'Tea?' he asked.

The detectives nodded.

'Shall I be mother?' said Callaghan.

'Three cups?' said Blizzard. 'Is Ray not joining us?'

'I think not,' said Callaghan.

'But we did request that–'

'You deal with me and me alone,' said Callaghan. The polite tone had been infused with a sharpness and the comment brooked no dissent. 'I can answer for Ray.'

'As you wish,' said Blizzard. 'We can always come back if we need to speak to him.'

Callaghan frowned but said nothing. He poured the last cup and slid a plate of biscuits across the desk.

'I take it that this is about Sergeant Steele?' he asked.

'You know it is, Nathaniel,' said Blizzard.

Callaghan's eyes narrowed; he was not used to being addressed by his Christian name; with police officers, it was usually 'Mr Callaghan' but then he already knew that John Blizzard was different. He was acutely aware that the inspector had already gained the upper hand in their encounter.

'And why do you wish to talk to Ray about it?' asked Callaghan.

'We know that he met Alan a few days ago,' said Blizzard.

'And how do you know that?'

Blizzard did not reply.

'I'm only toying with you,' said Callaghan. His turn to give a knowing smile. 'I imagine it was during a surveillance operation? We are being watched all the time. It really is rather tiresome.'

'I am sure that you don't expect me to confirm that,' said Blizzard.

'You don't need to. Suffice to say that I know everything there is to know about the surveillance. I imagine that the one that recorded Ray's meeting with Sergeant Steele was carried out by West Yorkshire Police on behalf of the National Crime Agency. They've got some fancy notion into their heads that I am planning to supply a group of Moroccans with firearms. All a misunderstanding, of course.'

Callaghan chuckled as the detectives exchanged glances.

'There is no need to try to hide it,' he said. 'I know it's supposed to be a big secret. You will, I imagine, be aware that your sergeant was in the company of a television producer who wishes to make a documentary about me? Just so as you are clear, I declined their offer. I do not like the idea of there being cameras everywhere when I am trying to work.'

Blizzard thought of his experience with the reality television team and nodded.

'That's something we can both agree on,' he said. 'Do you happen to know how Alan Steele got hold of Ray's mobile number?'

Callaghan gave a slight smile.

'I imagine you wish to ascertain if your officer was working for me. Well, he wasn't. My relationships with police officers tend to be at a rank above sergeant.' Callaghan glanced at Colley. 'No offence intended.'

'None taken,' said Colley. He felt the need to say something to show that the gangster's comment about his daughter had not unsettled him.

'Did you order the murder of Sergeant Steele?' asked Blizzard.

'Why would you think that?' said Callaghan. He feigned the impression that a thought had just struck him. 'Oh, I assume that you are referring to the Murder Gun?'

'I am,' said Blizzard. 'You have to admit that it's a–'

'Story created by a bored detective sergeant in Leeds many years ago,' said Callaghan. 'He got it into his head that it was used by a hitman that I hired from time to time to eradicate my rivals. The story is completely without basis, of course, as are many of the tales that are told about me. I am afraid that I am not half as interesting in real life as I am in legend.'

'What if I say that I think the gun does exist?' asked Blizzard.

'It's a fairy story,' insisted Callaghan.

'What if I don't believe you?' said Blizzard. 'And that I think you *did* order the death of Alan Steele and that I'm going to do everything in my power to prove it?'

'Belief and proof are very different things,' said Callaghan.

Irritation had flickered across his face and Colley held his breath; he knew that there were very real dangers if you pushed the gangster too hard, that the veneer of civility could easily shatter to reveal his true character. Callaghan regained his composure.

'Of course, you are free to believe what you wish,' he continued. 'But you can take it from me that I had nothing to do with the death of your officer.'

He gave Blizzard a hard look.

'And if you persist in contending that I *am* somehow involved, I will have to take action,' he said.

'What kind of action?' asked Blizzard.

'Let's just say that I have influential friends who take an interest in my well-being. Like I told you, one phone call and all this goes away.'

'Like Alan went away?' said Blizzard.

Callaghan's eyes glinted with fury but before he could reply, the office door opened and the secretary appeared.

'Your ten minutes is up,' she said.

Callaghan glanced at the wall clock.

'So it is,' he said and gave a slight smile. 'Time to go, gentlemen. People tend to defy Cynthia at their peril. Thank you for coming to see me. I trust that this will be the end of the matter.'

'You must believe what you wish,' said the inspector.

Callaghan frowned and the detectives stood up and Callaghan looked at the cups on the table. Neither drink had been touched.

'It's a pity you didn't have chance to finish your tea,' he said.

'Maybe next time,' said Blizzard.

'As I have already made clear, Chief Inspector, I sincerely hope that there will not be another time,' said Callaghan.

And he looked down at the document that he had been reading and picked up a pen. The audience was at an end.

## Chapter sixteen

It was another shaven-headed man who escorted the detectives out of the building. There was no sign of Ray Varone. Blizzard noticed David Colley breathe a sigh of relief as they emerged into the bright sunshine. If the inspector was honest with himself, he too was glad to be out of the building. It was clear that the gangster had been irritated by their visit and Blizzard knew that an irritated Nathaniel Callaghan was a dangerous Nathaniel Callaghan, and the image of Alan Steele on the table in the mortuary loomed large in the inspector's thoughts.

'So what do you think?' asked Colley as they got into the car. 'Did he order the murder?'

'I think there's a very real possibility that he did,' said Blizzard. He frowned. 'I'm not sure why, though.'

'To stop the documentary being made.'

Blizzard shook his head.

'Not sure he'd need to go that far,' he said. 'Nathaniel runs a tight ship and if he put the word out that he did not want anyone to talk to the TV people, it would take a brave person to defy him. No, there's something else, I am sure of it.'

'What do I do about Laura?' asked the sergeant. 'I mean, he knows what school she goes to, for God's sake.'

'He was just toying with you. I don't think he would do anything to harm her. He's got nothing to gain from doing something like that.'

'We'd have said the same thing about Alan,' replied Colley. 'How do I know that you are right?'

'We'll just have to be vigilant,' said the inspector. 'And I'd ring Jay. Just in case.'

It was not long before that vigilance was required because, as Blizzard guided his car away from the industrial estate, a black Audi with tinted windows pulled out of a side road and slotted in behind them. The vehicle stayed with the detectives as they made their way through the outskirts of the city, the Audi's driver keeping its distance behind several other vehicles. It was still there when Blizzard drove onto the motorway and headed east towards Hafton, where Colley glanced in the side mirror, something he had been doing with increasing frequency. The sergeant frowned.

'Call me paranoid…' he said.

'Which you are when it comes to Nathaniel Callaghan,' said Blizzard.

'You can't really blame me,' protested the sergeant. 'He knows which school my daughter goes to, for God's sake! However, what I was about to say was that–'

'We are being followed?'

Blizzard guided the car into the middle lane of the motorway in order to overtake a couple of slow-moving lorries and, as he did so, he noted that the black Audi had done the same.

'I'd say you were right,' he said.

Colley glanced in his side mirror.

'Two people, driver and passenger, but too far back for me to see their faces,' he said. 'Callaghan's men? Making sure we leave Leeds?'

The sergeant tried to make the question appear as casual as possible but could not conceal his nervousness.

'It's possible,' said Blizzard. He sounded much calmer than the sergeant. 'Except you'd think that they'd have lost interest once it became clear that we were heading for home. Can you read its numberplate?'

'No, it's too far back.'

'I'll slow down a bit so you can jot it down,' said the inspector.

A couple of minutes later, with the number duly recorded, Blizzard sped up again and the Audi resumed its position several cars back.

'Did you get a better look at them?' asked Blizzard.

'Not much better. Two men, short-hair. Young guys. In their twenties, I would say. I don't recognise them.'

The sergeant put a call in to the CID office at Abbey Road Police Station. The phone was answered by Sarah Allatt and Colley put her on speaker so that Blizzard could hear her response when he gave her the Audi's registration number. They could hear the constable typing on her computer keyboard.

'Now that's interesting,' she said after a few moments. 'According to the DVLA, it does not exist.'

'Well, it looks pretty real to me,' said Blizzard.

'The DVLA says it was scrapped three years ago.'

'So, what do you reckon?' asked Colley when the call had ended. 'If they're not Callaghan's men, who are they working for?'

'Could be anyone,' said Blizzard. 'Callaghan and his gang are under constant surveillance.'

'But wouldn't whoever it was know that this is your car and that we're the police?'

'Maybe they do, but if there were suspicions about Alan, maybe there are suspicions about us as well.'

'This is getting heavier by the minute.' Colley glanced in the side mirror yet again. 'So what do we do?'

'Sit tight for the moment. They don't look like they mean us any harm. But in the meantime…'

The inspector reached down to the cradle containing his mobile phone, scrolled down Contacts and clicked on a number.

'Traffic would be horrified,' said Colley with a slight smile. 'You've seen all the memos about using mobile phones when we're driving.'

'Somehow I think that Traffic are the least of our problems,' said Blizzard as the phone rang out.

'Hi, John,' said Wendy Talbot's voice. They could hear the low drone of a car's engine in the background as she and Riley continued to head south to London. 'How'd it go with Nathaniel?'

'As you might have guessed,' said Blizzard. 'Claims to know nothing about Alan's death. I'm ringing you because we've picked up a tail. You got a couple of your boys following us?'

'As if we would,' said Talbot. The detectives sensed that she was smiling. 'You got a registration number?'

Colley gave her the number.

'It's a black Audi,' he said. 'But they're fake plates.'

'It's definitely not one of ours,' said Talbot. 'Not one from West Yorkshire Organised Crime, is it, Matt?'

'Definitely not one of ours,' said Riley.

'OK,' said Blizzard. 'Leave it to me. I'll sort it.'

'I'm not sure I like the sound of that,' said Talbot. 'What are you going to do?'

'There's not much we can do until we're back in our own jurisdiction,' said Blizzard. 'But when we are, we'll have a nice welcome party waiting for them.'

The inspector ended the call. He had had enough of people playing games; it was time to take back the initiative. He glanced at Colley.

'See if Arthur's in, will you?' he said.

* * *

Little more than an hour later, the detectives' vehicle re-entered their force area with the black Audi still sitting half a dozen vehicles behind. Blizzard rang Ronald.

'You in position?' asked the inspector.

'We are,' said Ronald. 'We have you seven miles west of Junction 11?'

'That's about right,' said Blizzard.

'We'll hit them at the junction then. It's normally a quiet stretch of the motorway and it's well away from any houses.'

'Makes sense,' said Blizzard.

A few minutes later, they reached the sign for the junction and Blizzard glanced at Colley.

'Ready?' he said.

'Yeah,' said the sergeant. He gave a nervous smile. 'Feels kinda weird being on the other side of a stop.'

'Should be fun,' said Blizzard. 'As long as our guys don't shoot us by mistake, of course.'

Colley gave his boss a pained look.

'You really do have to work on your bedside manner,' he said.

Blizzard gave a slight smile but said nothing. As predicted by Ronald, the traffic had thinned out by the time the cars reached Junction 11 and now there were only two vehicles between the Hafton detectives and their tail, which allowed them to clearly see the stern features of the driver and his passenger. As the two cars passed the junction, three patrol vehicles headed down the slip road at speed to emerge behind them. One of the police cars pulled up close behind the Audi and the other two overtook it and slewed across the road, blocking it in. Before the startled occupants of the Audi were able to react, armed officers were out of all three police cars and had trained their weapons on their target.

'Get out of the vehicle!' shouted one of the armed officers.

For a few moments, there was no response from the men in the Audi so the firearms officer repeated his command. This time, the two men got out of the Audi.

'Hands where I can see them!' shouted the firearms officer.

The two men held out their hands and, within seconds, both had been handcuffed. Another patrol car headed down the slip road and came to a halt. Arthur Ronald got out and walked over to where Blizzard and Colley had left their vehicle and were studying the arrested men. Both were smartly dressed in dark suits that were all sharp creases.

'You recognise them?' asked Blizzard, glancing at Ronald.

The superintendent shook his head and was about to say something when one of the arrested men spoke.

'I would recommend that you let us go if you know what's good for you,' he said.

'Not until we know who you are and why you are following my detectives,' said Ronald. 'And I don't appreciate people telling me what's good for me. Who are you?'

'I can't tell you.'

'I beg to disagree,' said the superintendent. 'You see, I have a detective in the mortuary, a wife without a husband, two children without a father and you two tailing my officers. I would say that gives me every right to know.'

'One phone call and I can make this all go away,' said the man.

'Funny,' said Blizzard, glancing at Colley. 'That's exactly what Nathaniel Callaghan said to us earlier today, isn't it?'

Colley nodded and looked at the arrested men.

'Are you working for him?' he asked.

The man shook his head.

'Then who?' asked the inspector.

The man did not reply and Ronald looked at the armed officers.

'Take them to Abbey Road, please,' he said. 'We'll keep them in overnight and put them up before the magistrates in the morning.'

'Magistrates?' protested the man. 'On what charge?'

'Driving a vehicle that's unregistered, for starters,' replied the superintendent.

'I don't think you'd be that petty.'

'Don't be so sure about that,' said Ronald. 'Maybe the magistrate can persuade you to provide us with your names. And if not, we can always issue an appeal to the media with pictures of you both. *Do you know these men?*'

'OK, OK,' said the man as one of the armed officers took hold of his arm. He lowered his voice to speak in a conspiratorial tone. 'I'll tell you. We're with MI5.'

'Like I keep saying,' said Blizzard. 'It's getting more difficult to work out who are the good guys and who are the bad guys.'

# Chapter seventeen

Blizzard had not been long back in his office at Abbey Road Police Station, and had just sat down at his desk with a mug of tea, when Chris Ramsey walked in.

'I hear you've been playing nice,' he said as Blizzard gestured for him to take a seat. 'The atmosphere round this place is electric. Is it right that you've nicked a couple of Secret Squirrels?'

'Sure is.'

'Do we know why they were following you?' asked Ramsey.

'We're assuming that it must be something to do with Alan's death.' Blizzard shook his head. 'The more this case unfolds, the less I think I know about the man. First Nathaniel Callaghan and now MI5. Why would either of them be interested in a sergeant from Hafton?'

'No idea. Are the MI5 guys not saying anything?'

'They're sticking to the name and number routine,' said Blizzard. 'Not sure how long they'll keep it up, though. I think that they assumed that they would be released immediately once we found out who they were but the gravity of their situation may be starting to dawn on them. Arthur's been laying it on thick.'

'How long can we hold them, do you think?'

'Arthur's coming under all sorts of heavy pressure from their bosses to let them go, mind, but the chief is behind him for the moment so we're keeping them in until we get some answers. Even if we do let them go today, it won't be until much later. Wendy Talbot and Matt Riley want to be in on the questioning and are heading back north. Suffice to say that Wendy is not impressed – they weren't that far from London when this blew up.'

'I imagine she's furious,' said Ramsey. 'And I certainly wouldn't want to cross her. How did it go with Nathaniel? Did he agree that it's a fair cop and hand himself in?'

'What do you think? It was not the charming version of the man that we met this morning. I think we may have got him rattled.' Blizzard noted the piece of paper in the detective inspector's hand. 'What's that?'

'Something that may rattle him some more,' said Ramsey. He placed the document on the desk with a look of intense satisfaction on his face. 'In fact, it could be the first piece of evidence linking him with Alan's murder.'

'Really?' Blizzard picked up the document. It was a printout out of a DVLA record. He ran his eye down the page. 'Who's this Gary Race then?'

'Well might you ask,' said Ramsey. 'We got onto him after a delivery driver came into the front office and said he'd heard that we were appealing for information about Alan's murder. He said that he saw a car turn off towards the wasteland behind the new Tesco at about 8.30 on the night Alan vanished.'

'That's not long after he left the McDonald's,' said Blizzard.

'Exactly, and what makes it even more interesting is that the van driver jotted down the vehicle's registration number, which confirms that it's from Leeds.'

'If only everyone were as public-spirited,' said Blizzard.

'As you can see from the DVLA printout,' continued Ramsey, 'Gary Race lives in Leeds but we didn't turn up anything on criminal records.'

'So what do we know about him?'

'*We* don't know anything,' said Ramsey gleefully. 'But it turns out that we know a man who does.'

Blizzard gave a slight smile; Ramsey was usually such a dour character that it was a pleasant change to see him so enthused and his boss was enjoying the experience. Blizzard knew that the detective inspector had taken Alan Steele's death hard and decided to indulge him.

'And who might that be?' he asked.

'I rang West Yorkshire Police's Organised Crime Unit on the off-chance that they knew him. According to them, Race is one of Nathaniel Callaghan's trusted lieutenants. He first hooked up with him in Hafton when he was a young man. He's in his late fifties now. He's got a reputation as one of his enforcers – the type of man who may have access to the Murder Gun, one might think.'

'That's good work, Chris,' said Blizzard. 'Do we have anything apart from the van driver's statement to link him with the attack on Alan?'

'Roadside cameras have confirmed that his car headed into Hafton on the eastbound dual carriageway shortly after 8.30 and headed back less than half an hour later.'

'Just enough time to kill Alan.'

'Indeed. Unfortunately, the CCTV cameras on the Tesco building don't show the area down by the river, but the fact that we know he was near the turn-off at the time the van driver gave us should be enough to justify bringing Race in, shouldn't it?'

Blizzard thought for a few moments.

'Not yet,' he said. The inspector noted Ramsey's look of disappointment. 'I want us to be a hundred per cent sure before we move in on any of Callaghan's people, Chris. As Nathaniel was kind enough to remind us this morning, he has friends in high places and we'll only get one chance so I want us to be right.'

'Yes, but–'

'And I also want to know why MI5 were following us before we make our move. I can't afford to have us blundering in there and jeopardising someone else's investigation. MI5 have already got a low enough opinion of provincial police forces as it is.'

Ramsey looked suspiciously at his boss.

'Yes, well, I just hope that our investigation does not get kicked to the back of the queue,' he said. 'One of our officers is dead, in case people had forgotten.'

'I don't imagine that anyone has forgotten,' said Blizzard sharply. 'And I would suggest that you do not let anyone hear you saying it, either. Emotions are already raw enough round here.'

'Sorry,' said Ramsey. 'That was out of order but you can see why I'm concerned, can't you? It's like this every time we deal with national law enforcement organisations and I don't like it.'

'Me neither,' said Blizzard. Noting that Ramsey still looked disappointed, he adopted a more reassuring tone of voice. 'I'll not let us be sidelined, Chris. You have my word on that. I'll talk to Wendy Talbot when she gets here. See if we can use her influence.'

'Just so long as she's clear that this is our investigation,' said Ramsey. He stood up and headed for the door. 'We owe Alan that much.'

'I'll make sure to remind her,' said Blizzard.

Once Ramsey had gone, the inspector closed his eyes and sighed.

'God, how I hate politics,' he said wearily.

# Chapter eighteen

The atmosphere was tense in the interview room at Abbey Road Police Station early that evening. Arthur Ronald sat at the table, flanked on one side by John Blizzard and on the other by Wendy Talbot. All three of them were stern and unsmiling. Across the table was a slim short-haired woman in her mid-forties, sitting next to the two apprehended MI5 officers. Not that she would ever show it but Jane Kenworthy was acutely embarrassed to have been summoned to Hafton from London after her officers had been taken into custody. On arrival, she had made her views clear to her operatives in a short and terse conversation and now the two men sat silent and glum as they awaited the beginning of what threatened to be an uncomfortable encounter.

With so many people crammed into the small room, the heat was rising by the second and Blizzard noted with satisfaction that the oppressive atmosphere, combined with the gravity of their situation, was making both MI5 men sweat profusely. The inspector gave a slight smile; he liked it when suspects sweated and the initial bravado shown by the MI5 operatives had long since disappeared.

Jane Kenworthy focused her attention on Wendy Talbot, hoping that the detective's presence would give her half a chance of emerging from the situation with a few shreds of credibility – two women who had fought their way to the top of a man's world and all that. The MI5 officer hoped that they might be able to find a common bond in a room full of men. Talbot soon disavowed her of the notion.

'Well, this is a right royal cock-up, isn't it?' said the National Crime Agency officer, giving Kenworthy a hard look. 'All a bit Keystone Cops. I mean, it doesn't say much for the way your guys were trained that the lads clocked them within minutes, does it?'

'No, but–' began Kenworthy, but Talbot did not give her the chance to complete her sentence.

'Perhaps you would care to explain exactly why they were trailing two of Hafton's finest halfway across the north of England?' she said.

'Yes, perhaps you would,' said Ronald. 'I'm sure we would all like to hear your explanation.'

Kenworthy hesitated as she gathered her thoughts. The nature of her job meant that trust did not come easy to her and she did not trust any of the detectives. However, she also realised that she had been backed into a corner. Suspecting that would be the case, she had rehearsed what she was going to say numerous times as she drove north. As she did so, she bore in mind the words of her instructor when she left her job as a senior customs officer to join MI5 more than ten years previously: '*Always be what they expect you to be*,' he had said, '*that way they will never see the real you*.' It was time to play her part, decided Kenworthy.

'I'm sure you appreciate that this is a matter of national security,' she said. 'And as such, I am not able to divulge any informa–'

'Oh, cut the crap, Jane,' said Talbot. She looked at her colleagues. 'That lame old excuse won't wash with us.'

Ronald and Blizzard nodded.

'I am sure that I speak for all of us,' continued Talbot, 'when I say that we do not like the idea of MI5 tailing police officers, particularly given that they did it in such an incompetent manner. My four-year-old granddaughter could make a better job of it than they did.'

The arrested MI5 officers continued to stare down at the desk in cowed silence. Talbot's harsh words only added to those of their boss on her arrival at Abbey Road, her rebuke uttered in clipped tones as she warned them that their careers hung by a thread. Jane Kenworthy gave Talbot a gloomy look; this was not going the way she had hoped. She was about to speak when Arthur Ronald beat her to it.

'What happened earlier today is particularly alarming,' he said, 'because there is always an element of risk in armed operations and we do not like to carry them out when there's no good reason. Why was no one informed that our guys were under surveillance?'

Kenworthy looked at the resolute expressions on the other side of the table and gave a sigh.

'OK, OK,' she said. 'But I warn you, you're not going to like what I have to say. We did not inform anyone because we did not know who we could trust in Hafton Police.'

'What the hell does that mean?' asked Blizzard angrily.

'We have reason to believe that Detective Sergeant Steele was involved in some way with Nathaniel Callaghan and we need to know if the conspiracy involved other officers. That meant gathering information on your movements. When it became clear that you'd been to see Callaghan, we had no option but to follow you. You'd have done the same.'

'What made you think that Alan had connections with Callaghan anyway?' asked Blizzard.

'Because he met Ray Varone last week,' said Kenworthy. 'In a multistorey car park in Leeds.'

'Hang on,' said Talbot. She gave Kenworthy a suspicious look. 'That was *our* surveillance operation. How do you know about it? Were you watching *us* as well?'

'Not you,' said Kenworthy. 'Varone. Don't tell me that you didn't consider the possibility that Steele might have been corrupt when you saw that he had met him?'

'But didn't you wonder who the woman was who went with him?' asked Talbot.

'We thought she might be another police officer.'

'Well, she wasn't,' said Talbot. 'She's a television producer who wants to make a documentary about Callaghan.'

'A television producer?' said Kenworthy. She gave her officers a hard look. 'Why didn't we know that?'

Her colleagues shifted uncomfortably in their seats.

'And even if Alan was corrupt, why not let us handle it?' said Ronald. 'He was our man.'

'You're too close,' said Kenworthy.

'So if not Hafton Police, then why not us?' asked Talbot.

'It was felt that MI5 would be able to take a more independent line,' said Kenworthy. 'You're all police officers. Old loyalties die hard and this is a very sensitive matter. We believe that Nathaniel Callaghan has recruited a senior police officer to his payroll, someone who is keeping him fed with inside information about police investigations. It was not until your man Steele met Ray Varone that the pieces began to fall into place.'

'He was not corrupt,' said Ronald with a shake of the head. 'And for the record, our guys went to see Callaghan because we have reason to believe that he may be behind Alan's murder.'

'Yes, but we didn't know that.'

'You only had to ask,' said Blizzard and he stood up and left the room.

* * *

An hour later, with the two MI5 officers released without charge and they and Jane Kenworthy on their journey south, Blizzard was in his office with Talbot and Riley when Arthur Ronald walked into the room.

'How did it go with the chief?' asked Blizzard.

'Not well,' said Ronald. 'He does not appreciate one of his officers being accused of corruption. Particularly not one who can't speak up for himself.'

'What's he going to going to do about it?' asked Talbot.

'Nothing for the moment. He wants to see how it plays out.'

'And what about us?' said Blizzard. 'Are *we* going to wait to see how it plays out? I mean, we still go after Callaghan, yes?'

'We do, yes.'

'Excellent,' said Blizzard.

There was a knock on the door and Chris Ramsey walked in, holding a copy of *The West Hafton Community News*.

'Have you seen this?' he said, placing it on the desk.

Blizzard looked at the headline and sighed.

Mystery of dead policeman's last case, it read.

It was followed by an opening sentence beneath the word *Exclusive* and with the byline *Jenny Morton*, which said:

> *Murdered detective Alan Steele was working on a major case when he was gunned down, The West Hafton Community News can reveal.*
> *Police will not reveal the nature of the inquiry but they are believed to be linking it with his death, and to know more than they are prepared to admit.*

'Somehow I think she gives us too much credit,' said Blizzard. 'Like I keep saying, the more we learn about Alan, the less we know.'

# Chapter nineteen

The next day saw Blizzard and Colley back in Leeds, this time to attend an early morning briefing with the firearms team at one of the neighbourhood police stations. Once that had concluded, they headed in the inspector's car through deserted streets to the outskirts of the city, where Blizzard parked the vehicle in a pleasant, tree-lined avenue with a number of large, detached houses set back from the road. Sitting in the back seat of the car was one of the senior officers in the West Yorkshire Police Organised Crime Unit and, once Blizzard had cut the engine and switched off the lights, Colley turned round to look at him.

'Which one is Gary Race's house?' he asked.

'Halfway up on the left,' said Detective Inspector James Rowles. 'The one with the wrought-iron security gates.'

'Looks expensive,' said Colley. He peered through the shadows cast by the street lights and caught a glimpse of a gable end through the bare winter trees. 'Clearly, crime pays around here.'

Blizzard gave a slight smile.

'He says that whenever I take him somewhere nice,' he said. 'But he's right. It would seem that Race is making plenty of money.'

'They all are,' said Rowles. 'It's one of the reasons no one betrays Callaghan. He pays his people well so that they are not tempted to inform on him. Why derail the gravy train? He's one for psychology, is Nathaniel.'

'Presumably it also helps that, if they *do* cross him, they get to meet the man with the Murder Gun,' said Colley.

'I remain to be convinced about that,' said Rowles.

'What do you mean?' asked the sergeant.

'Nathaniel bumped off rivals early in his career, sure, but not for many years. He takes the view that it's too messy. That's why the Murder Gun has been out of circulation for so long.'

'So, you're saying that we are wrong about Gary Race?' said Blizzard.

'I'm saying the suggestion that Nathaniel had your sergeant killed does not make sense. He knows that killing a cop brings a heap of trouble, particularly if it's a famous one.'

'But you can't argue with the fact that Race's car was spotted in the area,' said Blizzard. 'Is it possible that he killed him without Nathaniel knowing about it? Maybe Varone set it up on his own?'

'Nothing happens without Nathaniel knowing about it,' said Rowles. 'Sorry, guys, I think you may be wasting your time. Anyway, here's the cavalry.'

He pointed to the two police minibuses that had turned in at the far end of the avenue and pulled up close to the target house. The doors opened to allow the firearms officers to disembark, which they did rapidly, moving with the practised ease that came with years of working together.

'Come on,' said Rowles. 'Let's get it over with.'

The detectives got out of the car and walked over to the gates, where they were approached by the leader of the firearms team. He glanced at the house, which was still in darkness.

'We're ready if you are,' he said.

'Go for it,' said Blizzard.

One of the police team walked forward with a hydraulic ram and smashed through the gates, allowing his colleagues to run up the gravel drive towards the detached house, where an upstairs bedroom light had been switched on. Another officer banged on the front door.

'Armed police!' he shouted.

After waiting for a couple of moments, he nodded at the officer with the hydraulic ram and, within seconds, the front door had gone in and firearms officers were streaming into the darkened hallway. Several of them clattered upstairs, shouting further warnings. From their position outside the house, the Hafton detectives heard a woman cry out in alarm followed by a man shouting angrily. It was all over in less than a minute and a man with thinning hair streaked with grey and wearing pyjama trousers and a T-shirt was brought down the stairs into the hallway by a couple of officers.

'Gary Race?' said Blizzard.

'Who wants to know?'

The inspector held up his warrant card.

'DCI Blizzard,' he said. 'Hafton Police.'

Race looked beyond the detectives to Rowles.

'What's the idea, James?' he asked. 'What do these jokers want?'

'To talk to you about the murder of one of their colleagues.'

'What, that cop shot dead in the warehouse?' said Race. 'What's that got to do with me?'

'Your car was spotted nearby at the time it happened,' said Blizzard.

'Not my car, pal.'

'Yes, your car,' said Blizzard. He glanced at a vehicle parked nearby. 'That one.'

'You've got it wrong,' said Race. 'I wasn't there.'

'There'll be plenty of time for that,' said Blizzard. 'Gary Race, you are under arrest in connection with the murder of Detective Sergeant Alan Steele. Read him his rights, Sergeant.'

Colley began to recite the oft-repeated mantra but Race interrupted him after a few words.

'This is crazy!' he exclaimed. He looked at Rowles. 'Tell him! I ain't never killed anyone. Tell him!'

'It's not my investigation,' said Rowles with the air of a man who did not wish to be dragged into the conversation. 'It's between you and DCI Blizzard.'

'Yes, and I don't intend to debate it here,' said Blizzard. He looked at Rowles. 'You got somewhere we can interview him?'

'I suppose so,' said Rowles.

As an officer began to lead Race away, he looked across at his wife.

'Tell Nathaniel what's happened,' he said. 'Tell him that I need help.'

'That's all we need,' said Rowles to Blizzard as Race was taken down the drive. 'Just remember that this was your idea. Keep me well out of it.'

Blizzard did not reply; it was not the first time he had heard such a comment from police officers when it came to Nathaniel Callaghan and such acquiescence had always concerned him. He wondered if the rumours were true that Callaghan had a senior officer in his pocket. The inspector, however, had no intention of coming over as similarly compliant and an hour later, he and Colley were back at the police station and seated in an interview room, staring across the desk at a defiant Gary Race, who was sitting with his arms crossed. His demeanour had not changed throughout the interview. Nor had his story.

'I keep telling you,' he said, 'you're wasting your time. I ain't been to Hafton for years. Whoever says they saw my car there got it wrong. I was at home all night. Just ask my wife.'

'But your car is on camera in Hafton,' said Blizzard. 'How do you explain that?'

'Someone set me up. I tell you, my car was parked on the drive at the time you said it was in Hafton.'

There was a knock on the door and a uniformed officer ushered in a thin, sallow-faced man who was immaculately dressed in a sharply pressed black suit with a folded handkerchief in the breast pocket despite the early hour. Blizzard tried not to straighten his own tie, which was at its customary half-mast position, but the compulsion was too strong. Colley noticed and smiled.

'This is Gerald Crabtree,' explained the officer. 'Mr Race's lawyer.'

'I understand that you have not charged my client,' said the lawyer. He did not sit down; he did not look pleased to be there at such an early hour and had the air of a man who had no intention of being in the interview room a second longer than was necessary. 'Is that the case?'

'Yes,' began Blizzard. 'But–'

'Do you intend to charge him?'

'I don't know at this stage,' said Blizzard. 'We hope that he is minded to help us with our inquir–'

'Mr Race is not minded to help you with anything,' said the lawyer tartly. '*Do* you have any evidence against him?'

'We can place his car at the scene.'

'They say they've got it on camera but it weren't me driving,' said Race. 'My car's been here all week and so have I. My missus will confirm that I've been around all the time. It's a stitch-up.'

The solicitor gave Blizzard a hard look.

'Do you have any other evidence?' he asked. 'If not, we will be leaving.'

Blizzard scowled; the inspector hated lawyers.

'Not at the moment,' he said. 'But…'

'In which case, it seems that you have arrested Mr Race on the flimsiest of pretexts,' said Crabtree. 'And you might as well know that he will not be answering any of your questions, however long you keep him here. Might I suggest that a better approach would be to release him until you have something more substantial? *If* you have something more substantial.'

Blizzard considered the comment for a few moments; faced with a lack of evidence, a prisoner who clearly was not going to co-operate and a local detective who thought that he was making a big mistake, the inspector was beginning to feel less and less sure of his position.

'I'll let him go if he undertakes not to leave the city,' he said.

Colley looked in surprise at his boss and Crabtree glanced at Race, who shrugged.

'I ain't going anywhere,' he said. He gave Blizzard a wicked smile. 'And I certainly ain't going anywhere near Hafton.'

Blizzard ignored the comment.

'And we'll want to examine your car,' he said.

'You won't find anything,' said Race.

Blizzard sighed; he suspected that Race was right. The inspector wafted a hand.

'OK, you can go,' he said.

Crabtree led the way out of the room, followed by a grinning Gary Race. When they had gone, Colley gave Blizzard a questioning look.

'What are you playing at?' he asked. 'Letting him go like that? We could have sweated him a bit longer, see if he gave anything up.'

'I don't think he would have given anything up,' said Blizzard. 'Assuming that he has anything to give up in the first place, that is.'

'You don't fancy him for the murder then?' said Colley.

Blizzard was about to say something when James Rowles walked in.

'You've let him go, then,' said the detective inspector. 'I'm not surprised, mind. Gerald Crabtree doesn't stand on ceremony.'

'Race is still of interest,' said Blizzard. 'Would your forensics people be prepared to examine his car for us?'

'I'd rather let your people come over to do it.'

'Why?'

'Like I said, I don't want to be involved more than I have to,' said Rowles. 'We only let you use our firearms guys because we didn't want to risk your people coming over to do it. Things could have got very sticky if it went wrong. There'd be a lot of flak flying – as it were.'

Blizzard looked at Rowles suspiciously.

'I thought you'd have jumped at the chance to nick one of Callaghan's trusted lieutenants?' he said. 'What's going on here, James?'

'There's a lot of politics surrounding Nathaniel Callaghan, as well you know. We have had our fingers burnt on several occasions. More than one career has come to an end because they crossed him.'

'This is ridiculous!' exclaimed Blizzard.

'Ridiculous it may be, but it's the way things are,' said Rowles as he headed for the door. 'Nice to have met you. Safe journey home.'

When he had left the room, the two Hafton detectives sat in silence for a few moments.

'There's a rabbit away here,' said Colley. 'Something we're not being told.'

Blizzard nodded and took his mobile phone out of his jacket pocket and dialled a number.

'Chris,' he said when Ramsey answered. 'Race is denying being in Hafton and I have this nasty feeling that he might be telling the truth. Can you get someone to check with the van driver? See if there's a chance that he *did* see who was behind the wheel?'

* * *

With the van driver not answering his mobile phone, Detective Constables Jenny Carr and Sarah Allatt were sent out to track him down. They arrived at the block of flats that he had given as his address shortly after 10.30am. The four-storey building stood behind a row of shops on one of the housing estates on the east side of the city and, having made their way up to the third floor, Carr rang on the doorbell of flat number thirty-one. There was no answer and they had just turned away having rung for the third time when a door on the other side of the landing opened and an elderly woman appeared.

'Are you looking for Brian Clifford?' she asked. 'Because you won't find him.'

'Why?' asked Carr.

'Why do you want to know?' said the woman.

The detectives showed their warrant cards.

'It's nothing to worry about,' said Carr. 'Just routine. Why won't we find him?'

'He hasn't been here for the best part of three months,' said the pensioner. 'In fact, the only time I saw him was the day that he moved in. I thought it was strange at the time.'

'Strange how?' asked Allatt.

'He didn't have any furniture,' said the pensioner.

* * *

Half an hour later, having contacted the housing association that owned the building, the two detectives were standing in the flat. The pensioner had been right; there was no furniture and the musty aroma in the air confirmed that no one had lived there for months. Carr rang Blizzard, who was heading towards his car with Colley as they prepared to head home.

'So there's no sign of him at all?' said the inspector once she had told him the news.

'If you ask me, he never lived here,' said Carr.

Blizzard ended the call.

'Do you know?' he said. 'With every second that passes, this case becomes ever more disturbing. Cops who won't move against Callaghan, witnesses who vanish and a detective sergeant with a bullet in his head, fired by a gun that everyone says is out of circulation.'

'So what's our next move?' asked the sergeant.

Before Blizzard could reply, his mobile phone rang again. He took it out of his coat pocket and looked at the words *Caller Unknown.* The inspector took the call.

'Blizzard?' said a voice that he recognised as Nathaniel Callaghan. 'You are starting to really annoy me. I had nothing to do with the death of your detective and neither did Gary Race. You had better stop telling people that we did.'

'Who told you–?'

'Just stop spreading lies,' said Callaghan.

'And what will you do if I refuse? Because I've seen what happened to Alan and–'

'Don't push your luck,' said Callaghan angrily.

The call ended abruptly and Blizzard put the phone back in his pocket.

'Spam call?' asked Colley.

'I'm not sure I like what he was selling, if it was,' said the inspector. 'No, that was Nathaniel Callaghan and he's not happy.'

'I assume he had your number from the last time we dealt with him?'

'Except I changed my phone, remember,' said Blizzard with a frown. 'After Mikey got yoghurt on it.'

Colley gave a slight smile at the memory of the inspector's irritation when he realised what had happened after he left the phone unguarded on the table where his son was eating his tea. The sergeant's smile did not last long as he realised the implication of what Blizzard had said.

'So, who gave him your new number?' he asked.

'I'm not sure that I want to think too hard about that,' said Blizzard. 'One thing's definite. We need to watch each other's back.'

'Was it not ever thus?' said the sergeant.

Blizzard gave him an affectionate look.

'Indeed it was,' said the inspector. 'Indeed it was.'

# Chapter twenty

Later that day, Blizzard was back in his office at Abbey Road Police Station, catching up on emails, when there was a knock on the door. He looked up from the computer with a sense of relief; he did not mind confronting villains but he detested tackling the immense amount of administration that accompanied his job running a busy CID department. He was surprised to see that his visitor was Sally Jackson. Standing at the door, the television producer looked somehow different, less confident, more vulnerable – frightened almost. John Blizzard was intrigued.

'Do you have a couple of minutes?' she asked in a quiet voice.

Blizzard gestured to the seat at the desk and she closed the office door and sat down. She sat in silence for a few moments as she gathered her thoughts and the inspector noticed how pale she had become.

'Do you want a glass of water?' he asked.

She shook her head.

'No, I'll be OK,' she said. 'I'm just really stressed.'

'The death of a colleague is a difficult thing to come to terms with.'

'It's not that.' She hesitated for a few moments, working out how to phrase her next sentence. 'Well, not entirely. You see, I am afraid that I have not been entirely honest with you.'

'Well, I'll go to the bottom of our stairs,' said Blizzard.

'What do you mean?'

'I mean that if I had a pound for every time someone said that to me, I'd be a rich man,' said the inspector. 'Just about everyone I meet tries to keep things from me but I tend to find out the truth in the end. Go on, tell all.'

'There's a rumour sweeping the station that you have arrested one of Nathaniel Callaghan's men for Alan's murder,' said Jackson.

'Is there now?'

'Yes. Is it true?'

'It is, yes, but we've had to let him go. We're having problems proving that he was over here on the night it happened.'

'But you think that he was?' she said.

'There's plenty of reason to believe so,' said Blizzard.

'So you are convinced that it was Callaghan who had Alan murdered then?'

'It's looking that way, but we're nowhere near proving it. There's no one more careful than Nathaniel Callaghan and getting people to provide information is always difficult. Can I assume that you know something that might help us?'

'I do, yes.' She glanced round nervously to make sure that she had closed the door properly and could not be overheard. 'But I don't want anyone to know that it came from me. I don't want to be the next one to die. Do I have your word on that?'

'It depends,' said the inspector. 'Does anyone else know what you are about to tell me?'

'Ray Varone certainly does.'

'So we can assume that he told Nathaniel then?'

Sally Jackson nodded miserably.

'I think it's why Alan was killed,' she said.

'In which case, you had better tell me everything you know,' said the inspector. 'Then maybe we can talk about arranging some protection for you.'

She gave him a grateful look.

'Thank you,' she said. 'I really would appreciate that.'

'So what *do* you know?'

'It's not what I know, it's what Alan knew. You see, when we went to Leeds, Ray Varone told us that it was highly unlikely that they would take part in the documentary. I thought that was the end of it. You can't really make a good film without the co-operation of the subject. In fact, Ray had turned to go, which was when Alan threatened him.'

Blizzard looked surprised.

'Threatened him?' he said. 'With what?'

'He told Ray that he already knew a lot about their activities and that we would make the film even if Nathaniel refused to take part. I was horrified; Alan had not warned me that he was going to say anything like that and it wasn't really his place anyway. I pride myself on being professional and would never do anything stupid like threatening a gangster, especially not a man like Nathaniel Callaghan.'

'It does not sound like the Alan Steele I know,' said Blizzard. 'Such behaviour is well out of character.'

'That's what I thought. He'd always come over as really calm and sensible. I was amazed.'

'Did he tell Varone what he actually knew about Callaghan?' asked the inspector.

'He wasn't specific, and he wouldn't tell me later either. Mind, neither of us said much on the journey back from Leeds. I was too angry with him. All he said was that he had his sources.'

'It wouldn't be difficult for him to find stuff out,' said Blizzard. 'Alan had access to all sorts of databases and it would be easy enough to find out the latest intelligence.

However, he would have known that using police intelligence for a film without permission would go against just about every regulation in the book.'

'And Alan wasn't the type to break the rules,' said Jackson. 'In my experience, he always played it straight.'

'It's why he was chosen to work with you. We knew that we could trust him, that he knew where the line was. Frankly, it beggars belief that he should act in the way you describe. Why would he take a risk like that?'

'He told me a couple of days before the meeting with Varone that he was desperate to get out of the police,' said Jackson. 'He saw the documentary as his big break. He said that Claire worried herself sick every time he went to work and that he was concerned about her health.'

'How did Varone react to all this?' asked Blizzard. 'I take it he was not impressed?'

'He was furious. He kept chewing his lip. He said that we were lucky that Alan had said it to him and not Nathaniel because he was not the sort of person to allow himself to be bullied. I had hoped that he would not tell Nathaniel what had happened but the next thing I knew, Alan had been murdered. It's hardly likely to be a coincidence, is it?'

'I wouldn't have said so.'

'I'm really worried that I may be next,' she said. Her voice trembled slightly and she gave Blizzard an anxious look. Tears glistened in her eyes. 'Nathaniel might assume that Alan had told me what he knew and that he has to silence me as well. I mean, that's possible, isn't it?'

'I am afraid it is,' said Blizzard. 'Whatever Callaghan thought that Alan knew, it must be big because he tends not to go round ordering the murder of police officers.'

'Tell that to Alan.'

'Indeed,' said Blizzard.

'And there's my team to think of as well,' said Jackson. 'They could be in danger as well. What do I tell them?'

'To stay vigilant.'

'Alan was vigilant and look what happened to him,' said Jackson. 'I was hoping that you could offer us something a bit more definite. Some protection, maybe.'

'I'll talk to Arthur,' said Blizzard. 'Maybe we can do something.'

'I'd be very grateful,' she said.

The producer slid her hand across the desk to briefly touch Blizzard's, a gesture that took the inspector aback. It was only the briefest of contacts but in that moment, he found himself attracted to the new, more vulnerable, Sally Jackson. The hard-headed producer of recent months seemed a distant memory. Blizzard's mind went back to the rumours about the affair with Alan Steele. If they had been true, he thought, if Alan *had* fallen for Sally Jackson, who could blame him for starting a relationship? She was an attractive woman, after all, and Alan did have a thing about redheads, if his wife was to be believed. As ever when the inspector considered such thoughts, he thought of Fee and Mikey and felt a stab of guilt. He noticed that Jackson was waiting for him to say something.

'But I am making no promises,' he said, trying to reassert some authority over a conversation in which he was aware that he had lost the initiative. 'Budgets are tight. But I'll ask.'

After Jackson had gone, it was a pensive detective who walked along to Arthur Ronald's office and took a seat at the desk.

'How goes it?' asked the superintendent.

'We're getting there,' said Blizzard. 'Although I'm not quite sure where "there" is.'

He recounted the conversation with Sally Jackson, at the end of which the superintendent frowned.

'It doesn't sound like the Alan Steele I knew,' he said.

'Nor me,' said Blizzard. 'However, it does fit in with the suggestion that the older Nathaniel gets, the more paranoid he becomes.'

'He is seventy-two,' said Ronald. 'He can't go on for ever.'

'Indeed he can't,' said Blizzard. The inspector's eyes gleamed. 'This could be our big chance to get him, Arthur. Do what no one else has been able to do. Maybe the old man is beginning to make mistakes.'

'Maybe he is but do we trust Sally Jackson? Is she telling the truth?'

'I think she may be,' said Blizzard. 'She's become a lot more co-operative since she decided that she needs protection.'

'Yes, well, I hope that you did not promise anything.'

'I told her I would talk to you but that finances are tight.'

'That's the understatement of the year,' said Ronald gloomily. He picked up a bulky file from the desk then dropped it back down with a resounding thud. 'I've just received the budget for next year. It's seventy-six pages but it could just as easily be one page with the word "no" on it.'

Blizzard chuckled.

'That bad, eh?' he said.

'That bad,' said Ronald. 'And I very much doubt that it extends to providing protection for film crews.'

'Even if Nathaniel Callaghan is the prize?'

'It's certainly an intriguing thought,' said Ronald. 'What's our next move?'

'Tricky, that's what it is.'

'Like all the others haven't been?' said Ronald, giving his friend a bleak look. 'We've already pissed off MI5, got West Yorkshire Police twitchy about our activities in their area and ruffled Nathaniel Callaghan's feathers. Who do you want to piss off next?'

'I want to arrest Ray Varone,' said Blizzard. 'See what he knows.'

'Why not go the whole hog and lift Callaghan as well?'

'Not yet,' said Blizzard. 'Nathaniel has always regarded himself as untouchable so I think that the best tactic for the moment is to isolate him. Arresting the likes of Race and Varone will let him know that we are not afraid to go after him.'

'There'll be a lot of politics. I hope you're prepared for that?'

'When did politics ever worry us?'

'It might not worry you,' said Ronald. 'But it plays merry hell with my ulcer.'

Blizzard gave his old friend an affectionate look; he had lost count of the number of times they had had the same conversation since they were reunited at Abbey Road Police Station but Ronald had always found a way of making things happen.

'You love it really,' said the inspector.

Ronald grunted.

'I'll make some calls,' he said.

'Good man,' said Blizzard.

The inspector was making his way back to his office when Colley approached along the corridor.

'I've just come off the phone from Gary Race's missus,' said the sergeant. 'She has confirmed that he was at home on the night Alan was killed.'

'I'd be amazed if she said anything different. Do you believe her?'

'I'm not sure,' said Colley. 'It would have helped if Versace's people found anything when they examined Race's car in Leeds but they came up blank. Did Arthur give us permission to go after Varone?'

'He said he'd have to check with his ulcer,' said Blizzard.

# Chapter twenty-one

The next morning found Blizzard and Colley back in Leeds once more, where they attended another pre-dawn briefing with the firearms team at the same police station that had been used before the raid on Gary Race's home. Also present was Detective Inspector James Rowles from the Organised Crime Unit, a glowering presence sitting at the back of the room. Standing at the front, next to the firearms team leader, Blizzard tried to ignore Rowles's frequent frowns but inevitably his self-restraint began to fail him and he found himself growing increasingly irritated.

Leaning against the wall as usual, Colley noted his boss's darkening demeanour with concern, and sighed. The sergeant knew that look and the explosion could not be far away; John Blizzard was not a man to shy away from conflict. Colley was not wrong – the two men had worked together for long enough for that ever to be the case – and the inspector finally lost his temper after Rowles fell into step with the Hafton detectives as they followed the firearms officers out of the room following the briefing.

'I hope you know what you're doing,' said the detective inspector as they headed along the corridor in the direction of the yard behind the station. 'Lifting Gary Race is one thing but Ray Varone takes it to the next level. You're moving into the big league.'

'Maybe we are,' said Blizzard. He tried to remain calm despite being irritated by the patronising comment. 'However, we are perfectly capable of handling someone like Ray Varone and we really do need him to confirm that Alan threatened to expose Callaghan.'

'Your guy would be a very silly boy if he did,' said Rowles.

'Well, he's a very silly, *dead* boy,' said Blizzard, pointedly. 'And we need to know why.'

'Look,' said Rowles. 'I appreciate that you've lost a man, and I sympathise, really I do, we all do, but you're wasting your time. I've never known Varone to say anything to the police in all the years I have dealt with him. Every time we have brought him in, the interview has been "no comment". You'll not get anything out of him.'

'We'll see,' said Blizzard in a tone of voice that suggested that he had had enough of the conversation.

'Suit yourself,' said Rowles. 'But don't say that you weren't warned.'

Blizzard stopped walking and turned to face Rowles, a furious look on his face.

'What's your problem?' he said angrily. Noticing that a couple of firearms officers had turned to look at them, the inspector lowered his voice. 'We have the best chance in years of bringing Nathaniel Callaghan before a court and all you can do is throw barriers in our way. Maybe *you're* the bent copper that MI5 keep talking about.'

Rowles noticed the interest being shown by the firearms officers and motioned towards an empty office.

'In there,' he hissed.

Once they were in the room and the detective inspector had closed the door, he gestured to the seats at the desk.

'Sit down,' he said.

'What–?' began Blizzard.

'Just sit down and shut up!' said Rowles.

The Hafton detectives did as instructed and waited in silence as Rowles walked over to the window and took a few moments to gather his thoughts.

'I know that MI5 believe Callaghan has got a senior officer on his payroll,' he said. 'Well, it's not me and I resent the suggestion that it is.'

Rowles angrily jabbed a finger in Blizzard's direction.

'I deserve better than that,' he said.

Always a man who relied heavily on instinct, Blizzard sensed that the detective was telling the truth and that the anger was genuine.

'I apologise,' he said. 'I reacted the same way when MI5 suggested it might be us.'

'The trouble is that they've got everyone looking suspiciously at each other and it's not healthy,' said Rowles. He gave a slight smile. 'Bravo for the way you dealt with them, anyway.'

The Hafton detectives returned the smile and the tension in the room eased.

'So in this new spirit of *entente cordiale*, are you going to tell us what on earth is happening with Ray Varone?' asked Blizzard.

'Yes, but whatever you do, don't tell MI5. It may be a new era of openness but the last thing I want is them buggering things up. Do you promise?'

The Hafton detectives nodded. They had little difficulty in acceding to the request.

'OK then,' said Rowles. 'I suppose that I can't really blame you for being suspicious about me. And you're right, I don't want you to arrest Ray. Not yet, anyway.'

'Why not?' asked Blizzard.

'Because he's working for us.'

Blizzard and Colley stared at him in amazement.

'Ray Varone is an informant?' said Blizzard.

'He is, yes. If you have been talking to Wendy Talbot and Matt Riley, you'll know that the National Crime

Agency is concerned about the deal that Callaghan has been negotiating to supply weapons to a Moroccan gang?'

The Hafton detectives nodded.

'Well, what they won't have told you is that the initial information came from us,' said Rowles. 'And that we got it from Ray. He came to us several months ago. Said it went against everything be believed in but that he was prepared to work with us. We passed it onto the NCA, which is why Matt was seconded to work with Wendy; he knows more about Callaghan's gang than just about anyone.'

'But why on earth would Varone turn informant?' asked Colley.

'Because he wants something. He is violently opposed to working with the Moroccans and wants us to get them off his back.'

'What's he got against the Moroccans?' asked Colley. 'I would have thought that they are exactly his kind of people?'

'The Moroccans did a similar deal six months ago with a gang in Germany,' said Rowles. 'But once the firearms had been delivered, they invited the leaders to a restaurant to celebrate and gunned down the lot of them. Seven of them died and one's in a wheelchair for life.'

'That was them, was it?' said Blizzard. He recalled how, when he watched the television news reports, he had thought with some relief that, however bad Hafton's criminals were, they were not capable of outrageous acts like that. 'Heavy stuff.'

'Yes, and far too heavy for Ray. Not surprisingly, he is worried that he and Nathaniel will go the same way.'

'What's Callaghan's take on it?' asked Blizzard. 'Does he not agree?'

'Apparently not. According to Varone, even though Callaghan has dealt with some right crackerjacks down the years, he has always been very careful about who he trusts. Varone says that on this occasion, though, he's not listening to the warnings. Varone says it is the latest in a series of poor decisions that Callaghan has made. He has become convinced that the old man is losing his grip, trusting the wrong people and putting the whole gang at risk. He even told me that he thinks Callaghan may be in the early stages of dementia.'

'He didn't look like he had dementia when we met him,' said Colley. 'He looked pretty sharp to me, didn't he, guv?'

'He did,' said Blizzard.

'Varone reckons he covers it well,' said Rowles, 'but that he knows what is happening to him. Anyway, Varone is going to set up a meet with the Moroccans in the next few days at which they will expect to take delivery of the guns. Instead, they'll find the NCA there along with some of our guys.'

'But surely the Moroccans will work out who betrayed them?' said Colley. 'It wouldn't take a genius and then Callaghan and Varone will be for the high jump.'

'Varone has asked us to issue a statement to the press afterwards saying that the tip-off came from an informant in Morocco.'

'I can't see that fooling anyone,' said Blizzard.

'Ray seems to think it will,' said Rowles. 'He says that the Moroccans are even more paranoid than Nathaniel and that none of them trust each other. He reckons it'll spark a civil war between those gang members that do not get lifted and that they'll probably end up killing each other.'

'But won't you have to arrest Callaghan and Varone as well?' asked Colley.

'Not necessarily. Callaghan will not be there at the handover of the weapons – he never is – and we'll release Varone pending further investigation and let it drop when the time is right.' Rowles gave a slight smile. 'It wouldn't be the first investigation into them to do that, would it now?'

'I guess not,' said Blizzard. 'Meanwhile, Ray Varone gets what he wants. The Moroccans off his back.'

Rowles hesitated.

'It's more complicated than that,' he said eventually.

'Now why I am not surprised?' said Blizzard. 'Go on, do tell.'

'Varone hopes that the collapse of the arms deal will convince Callaghan that he's getting too old for this kind of thing and that he should stand aside and let Ray take over.'

'I can't see his sons letting that happen,' said Blizzard.

'They've both been in and out of hospital,' said Rowles. 'Varone reckons they won't need much persuading as long as he sees them right. He's got it all worked out.'

'What do West Yorkshire Police get out of it?' asked Blizzard. 'NCA will grab all the glory for preventing the Moroccans carrying out a bloodbath on British streets. You know what they're like.'

'Yes, I know, but I keep telling myself that, although Ray is not exactly Mother Teresa, he will be much easier to deal with than an unstable Nathaniel Callaghan, especially if he keeps feeding us information.'

'And will he?' asked Blizzard.

'He says he will,' replied Rowles.

'Only on his terms, I imagine,' said the inspector. 'Don't you feel uncomfortable at the thought that you are helping him? You're treading very close to the line.'

'I know, I know,' said Rowles with a sigh. 'It doesn't exactly sit well with me. Anyway, things were already complicated enough before Alan Steele and the woman from the television company turned up. According to Ray Varone, that really spooked Nathaniel and your arrival on the scene has not helped either, John. Callaghan is very wary of you.'

'He's right to be,' said Blizzard. 'I mean, we can't ignore the suggestion that he set up the murder, can we?'

'Not really,' said Rowles. 'I could have done with a few extra days before you brought Varone in, though.'

'Sorry, but I'm hoping that he will confirm it was Callaghan,' said Blizzard.

'I doubt he will,' said Rowles. 'He has made it clear that he'll only talk to us and we've told him that we have nothing to do with your investigation.'

'Does he know that we're coming for him?' asked Blizzard.

'We certainly haven't told him.' Rowles looked down into the yard and noticed that the firearms team had climbed into their minibus and that their leader was looking up at him and tapping his wristwatch. 'Come on. We'd better be off.'

The Hafton detectives followed him along the corridor and, as they did so, Colley deliberately lagged behind Rowles. When the sergeant was sure that the detective inspector could not hear him, he said in a low voice, 'So tell me again, who are the good guys?'

'Fuck knows,' replied Blizzard.

# Chapter twenty-two

Thirty minutes later, the three detectives were standing in a pleasant tree-lined avenue on the outer fringes of the city, watching the firearms team go through its oft-practised drill as they approached a detached mock-Tudor house at the end of a long gravel drive. As the officer with the hydraulic ram approached the front door, the lights went on in the house and the front door swung open to reveal Varone, who was already dressed in jeans and a leather jacket. An overnight bag was at his feet.

'Good morning, gentlemen,' he said calmly, his voice a mixture of broad Yorkshire and a hint of Italian. He gestured to the firearms. 'And put them away, for God's sake. You'll end up hurting someone.'

The firearms team members looked confused and several of them turned to seek guidance from Blizzard.

'You would appear to have been expecting us,' said the detective, his lips pursed. He glanced at Rowles. 'I wonder how that happened?'

'Nothing to do with me,' said Rowles. 'Who tipped you off, Ray?'

'You don't need to know,' said Varone. He picked up his bag. 'Shall we go? Get it over with? It shouldn't take long.'

The surprise that the detectives had experienced when the front door swung open was nothing when compared with the turn of events back at the police station. Having taken Varone into an interview room, Blizzard and Colley prepared themselves for the gangster's stonewalling but he was the one who spoke first, looking at Rowles as he did so.

'Can I trust them?' he asked.

Rowles nodded.

'In which case, I'll tell you what I know about the murder of your detective,' said Varone. 'But on one condition – that you don't tell Nathaniel that I talked to you.'

'Won't he work it out anyway?' asked Blizzard.

'He might do but thinking it and proving it are two very different things and he can't risk falling out with me, the way things are. Ask your questions but I won't be making a statement and I won't stand up in court. I'm only doing this because James asked me to.'

Still unsure that he believed in the idea of a co-operative Ray Varone, Blizzard looked at Colley, who raised an eyebrow. *I have no idea what's happening anymore*, said the sergeant's expression. *Is he one of the good guys or one of the bad guys?*

'OK,' said the inspector. 'We have been told that Alan Steele was killed because he threatened to expose Nathaniel in a documentary. Is that true?'

'It is, yeah. He said that he'd already got a lot of information on us and that they'd make the film whether we were involved or not. He was very aggressive about it. The girl looked really shocked. I don't think she knew that he was going to say it.'

'Did Alan tell you what information he was referring to?' asked the inspector.

'Not specifically but he's a copper, he can get hold of all sorts, can't he?'

'He can, yes,' said Blizzard. 'And when you told Nathaniel what he'd said. What was his reaction?'

'He was furious,' replied Varone. 'Said that we couldn't risk them going ahead with it. I told him that we should ignore them, and the Nathaniel Callaghan of five years ago would have done so, but he seemed really worried. Kept saying over and over again that we had to stop them.'

'And did he say how he proposed that you should stop them?' asked Blizzard.

'I think you know the answer to that. Otherwise, you wouldn't be here, would we?'

'For the avoidance of doubt?'

'He said that we should kill Alan Steele.'

The sentence was delivered in such a matter-of-fact, off-hand manner that Colley could not stop himself muttering a curse beneath his breath. Blizzard gave him a look and the sergeant mouthed the word 'sorry'.

'And what did you say?' asked Blizzard.

'I said I wouldn't have anything to do with it,' said Varone. 'I don't like any of you, never have, but I'm not stupid. I know that killing a copper brings a heap of trouble down on your head, particularly someone who was well-known off the telly. And I've been proved right, haven't I?'

'Who carried out the shooting?' asked Blizzard. 'Was it Gary Race? His car was spotted in the area where the murder took place.'

'Then it must have been him, mustn't it?'

'Except his wife confirms his story that he was at home all that night.'

'Would you expect her to say anything else? If he gets locked up for murder, she loses her nice lifestyle, doesn't she?'

'Did he carry out the other murders as well?' asked Blizzard. 'The ones all those years ago?'

Varone shrugged his shoulders.

'Come on, Ray,' said Blizzard. 'Don't tell me that you don't know who it was.'

'I don't.'

'I don't believe you.'

'Believe what you want,' said Varone. 'But only Nathaniel knows who uses the gun. I didn't even know that he still had it. But one thing I do know is that he wanted Steele dead.'

'What about Sally Jackson?' asked Blizzard. 'Is she in danger as well?'

'Nathaniel seemed more worried about the copper. Said he was the one who could get hold of the information but I wouldn't rule out him going for her as well. He's losing his grip. Becoming more paranoid with every day that passes.'

Silence settled on the room as the detectives considered what they had been told.

'So what happens now?' asked Varone. He looked at Rowles. 'If they arrest me, you can say goodbye to our little arrangement.'

Rowles looked worried and Blizzard shook his head.

'I'm not going to arrest you, Ray,' he said. 'I am regarding you as an informant, not a suspect.'

Rowles heaved a sigh of relief.

'Are you going to arrest Nathaniel?' asked Varone.

'I'm not sure we have enough to make a charge stick,' said Blizzard. 'Especially if you decline to make a statement.'

Varone stood up.

'I'm sure you'll find a way round it,' he said. 'You seem to be a resourceful man.'

And with that he picked up his bag from the floor and looked at Rowles.

'You going to get someone to take me home, James?' he said.

Rowles nodded and the two men left the room.

'What do you think?' asked Colley.

'That we're not much further on,' said Blizzard. 'I think that Ray Varone is playing games. He sees us as another way of distracting Callaghan. I mean, without his written statement, what do we have? Gary Race was in Hafton? Well, we can prove that his car was, or at least one bearing its plates, but we can't prove that he was driving it, can we? Callaghan said he wanted to kill Alan? Sure, but we have no proof that he actually said it or that he followed through on it. Certainly not enough to put in front of the CPS.'

The inspector stood up.

'Come on, let's get back to Hafton,' he said, 'I need to take a trip down memory lane.'

* * *

Having returned to the city, Blizzard dropped Colley off at Abbey Road Police Station and went to see Charles Radley again. The old man opened the door and beamed a welcome.

'Twice in two days. I am honoured,' he said.

Once they were seated with mugs of tea, the retired police officer gave a slight smile.

'Still want me to solve your murder for you?' he said.

'Something like that. I wanted to run a name past you. Gary Race. He lives in Leeds but has Hafton connections. I wondered if you ever came across him in your days on the force. He may well have been knocking round with Nathaniel Callaghan.'

'He did indeed,' said Radley. 'Bit of a bully boy. He followed Nathaniel over to Leeds, as I recall. Why so interested?'

'We are thinking that he may be the one who uses the Murder Gun.'

Radley shook his head.

'Sorry, John,' he said, 'but I'm not sure I can see that. Race was handy with his fists but I don't buy him as a hitman. You got any firm evidence?'

'It's mainly circumstantial.'

'Call it instinct,' said Radley, 'but I don't think Gary Race is your man.'

Blizzard sighed.

'I fear,' he said, 'that you may be right.'

# Chapter twenty-three

Blizzard had been back in his office for twenty minutes when Fee walked into the room, accompanied by Michael, who toddled along happily at her side, gripping a bedraggled teddy bear in his hand. Fee had actually been at the station for half an hour but, although she had big news to impart to Blizzard, it had taken her all that time to make her way from reception to the inspector's room as former colleagues kept waylaying her to catch up on her news and say hello to Mikey. More than ten years younger than Blizzard, she had met the inspector when she was transferred to Western CID several years previously. Having taken maternity leave, she decided that balancing CID work and caring for a young child were incompatible so took a job with a security company which offered more regular hours. However, the job did occasionally take her back into her former world.

Mikey gave a yelp of delight when he saw his father sitting behind the desk and Blizzard beamed and walked over to lift him into the air, at which the young boy gave another squeal. The inspector placed him back on the floor then gave Fee a kiss on the cheek.

'What brings you here?' he asked.

'I've got something that may interest you,' she said. 'About Alan's murder.'

Blizzard was about to reply when Mikey reached up onto the desk and grabbed the stapler.

'I think not, young man,' said the inspector quickly. He took the stapler off the child, removed a couple of Biros from the pen holder and handed the toddler a document from his in-tray.

'Here,' he said, handing the pens to his son, 'draw on that.'

'Isn't it important?' asked Fee as her son settled down on the floor and started to produce a series of extravagant swirls across the document's glossy front page. 'It looks like it is.'

'It's just something from HR,' said Blizzard. 'Yet another strategy. What's this thing that may interest me, then? I hope it's good because I'm getting nowhere.'

'Oh, it's good alright,' said Fee. Her eyes were gleaming with anticipation at his reaction as she produced a laptop from her shoulder bag, placed it on the desk and called up a file. 'Take a look at this.'

She tapped the keyboard and Blizzard watched the film that had been recorded on a stretch of dual carriageway that he instantly recognised as the eastbound approach to the Tesco supermarket. It was dark and traffic was light.

'It was taken on the dashcam of one of our patrol guys the night Alan was murdered,' said Fee. 'He'd have come forward earlier but after he finished his shift, he caught an early morning flight to Spain on a short golfing break so only heard about the murder when he got back today.'

'What am I looking for?' asked Blizzard.

'You'll see,' said Fee. She pointed to the screen. 'There.'

Blizzard watched as a slim figure dressed in black, with their head concealed beneath a hood and carrying a holdall, emerged from bushes on the roadside, checked that the road was clear then ran over to the central reservation. The figure seemed nervous and hesitated for a few moments before darting across the road in the direction of the supermarket and disappearing off-screen.

'Interesting,' said Blizzard.

'I thought so.'

The inspector glanced at the digital readout on the footage.

'It fits in with the time we think Alan was arriving at the car park,' he said. 'Can you run it again, please?'

'Sure,' said Fee.

She tapped the keyboard, allowed the footage to run then froze the image. Blizzard leaned forward to examine the figure.

'Pity we can't make out the face,' he said. 'As it stands, it doesn't take us much further forward.'

'Au contraire, *mon cherie*,' said Fee. 'For starters, it's a woman.'

'Yeah?' Blizzard looked closer. 'Are you sure?'

'I am,' said Fee. 'And what's more, I think I've just seen her in the corridor!'

* * *

'So are we saying that Sally Jackson is a suspect?' asked David Colley. The sergeant's sceptical tone of voice suggested that he would require a lot of convincing.

It was late afternoon and he and Chris Ramsey had been summoned to Blizzard's office.

'I'm not sure,' said Blizzard. 'But whether she is or not, she needs to explain what she was doing there on the night that Alan was killed, doesn't she? Did you check her background, Chris? I take it that she *did* go through a security check before they started filming?'

'They all did,' said the detective inspector.

'And?'

'And nothing,' said Ramsey. He glanced at the document resting on his knee and ran his finger down the list of names. 'A couple of the cameramen had driving bans for speeding but that's all. Nothing came up when they checked out Sally Jackson.'

'Did they look at her CV as well?'

'They did, yes, but they didn't turn up anything to worry about,' said Ramsey. He switched his attention to another piece of paper. 'She's thirty-six and worked for a couple of other independent TV companies before joining Smoking Gun in 2015, initially as a producer specialising in true crime reality shows. *Community Fightback* is her baby. She became a company director eighteen months later, responsible for new projects. Oh, and she won a Royal Television Society award for a show on rural crime with Lincolnshire Police in 2020. Your old neck of the woods, guv.'

'I remember it,' said Blizzard. 'They filmed quite a lot of it in the area that I lived as a child. Anything on her on soft intelligence?'

Ramsey shook his head.

'Nothing,' he said. 'I know that camera footage puts her at the scene but I don't see her as a killer. For a start, Alan was her golden boy. Why on earth would she want to see him killed?'

'Do you have another theory?' asked Blizzard.

'That they *were* having an affair,' said Ramsey. 'That she was the person who Alan was talking to on his mobile when he was in the McDonald's car park. That she arranged to meet him there.'

'Very romantic,' said Blizzard. 'Nothing like the sweet aroma of pigeon droppings to set the mood for love, I find.'

'Maybe they wanted somewhere they would not be seen,' said Ramsey. 'Alan was pretty well-known because of the TV programme, remember, so going to a restaurant or a pub was pretty risky. Someone would be bound to see them and it wouldn't be long before it turned up on Facebook.'

'So what are we saying?' replied Blizzard. 'That she was in the wrong place at the wrong time? That Callaghan's man tracked Alan to the warehouse, waited for her to leave then killed him?'

'It would explain why she did not tell us she was there,' said Ramsey. 'She'd want to keep the affair secret. Like she told you, she wouldn't want to be seen to have done anything that would jeopardise the company's agreement with the force.'

Blizzard considered the idea then nodded.

'OK, I'll buy it,' he said. 'But I don't want to discount her as a suspect just yet.'

'So what do we do now?' asked Colley. 'Interview her?'

'Not yet,' said Blizzard. 'No, we need more evidence before we do that. You have seen the kind of trouble she can cause if she thinks she is being victimised.'

'What are we doing about Nathaniel Callaghan?' asked Ramsey. 'He's still in the frame for it, isn't he?'

'He is, yes,' said Blizzard. He thought for a few moments then came to the decision with which he had been wrestling. 'OK, let's bring him in for questioning.'

'Arthur will love that,' said Colley just as the office door swung open and the superintendent walked in.

'Love what?' he asked. 'And it's Superintendent Ronald to you.'

'Oops,' said the sergeant.

'And what won't I li...?' began Ronald. The superintendent's voice tailed off as he noticed the HR document lying on the desk, its front page covered in Michael's scrawls from earlier that afternoon. He gave Blizzard a stern look. 'I do hope that's not the new Force Diversity Strategy?'

'It is indeed,' said Blizzard.

'And what, pray, is that on the cover?'

'I am reliably informed that it is a frog wearing a top hat while standing on the top of a hill,' said Blizzard. 'If you ask me, I would say that young Mikey has a glittering career in graphic design ahead of him. It's better than the rubbish our people come up with.'

'You may be right there,' said Ronald. He returned his attention to Colley. 'Anyway, what won't I like?'

'That I want to bring Nathaniel Callaghan in for questioning,' said Blizzard.

'Are you sure that he had Alan killed?' asked the superintendent.

'No.'

'Do you have any evidence to suggest that he might have been involved in some way?'

'No.'

'Is there anything else you wish to say in support of your request?' asked Ronald.

'No.'

Ronald frowned.

'It's not the most persuasive case that you have ever brought to me,' he said.

'I appreciate that,' replied Blizzard. 'But we've got to start to make sense of this, Arthur. And if we bring him in, it will give us a chance to rule him out of our investigation, at the very least.'

'Rule him out?' said Ronald. He looked at his friend in surprise. 'I thought Ray Varone told you that he was behind the killing?'

'He did,' said Blizzard. 'But I'm not convinced that he was telling the truth. He's got his own agenda, has Ray Varone. It's entirely possible that he's framing him for Alan's death.'

'But what about the Murder Gun?' asked the superintendent. 'That links directly back to Callaghan, doesn't it? And if he is not responsible for Alan's murder, who is?'

'It's possible that the answer is to be found much closer to home,' said Blizzard. 'See, we have a theory but you're not going to like it. And it will mean you authorising us to do a spot of burglary tonight.'

'Which reminds me,' said Ronald. 'I need to pop in to the pharmacy for my ulcer medication!'

# Chapter twenty-four

'This feels very wrong,' said Colley as he placed the key in the door lock. 'Shouldn't we have a warrant or something?'

'Why?' said Blizzard. 'It's our police station.'

'Yes, but it's not our office, is it?'

'Just unlock the door,' said Blizzard.

It was shortly before 8pm, Abbey Road Police Station was largely deserted, its corridors dimly lit and silent, and the two officers were standing outside the television company's office.

'You're the boss,' said the sergeant.

'And don't you forget it,' said Blizzard.

Colley turned the key and Blizzard took his mobile phone out of his pocket and dialled a number.

'All clear, Chris?' he said.

'All clear,' said the detective inspector.

The detectives entered the room and Blizzard closed the door and switched on the light. They stood in silence for a few moments, surveying the room. Nothing leapt out as unusual.

'What are we looking for?' asked Colley.

'I don't know.'

'I'll look for one of them then,' said the sergeant.

It did not take the officers long to check the drawers in the desks but they found nothing of interest, until Blizzard tried the last one, which was locked. The photograph on the top of the desk showed Sally Jackson holding her Royal Television Society award and standing outside a police station which Blizzard recognised as Gainsborough in Lincolnshire. He gestured to the drawer.

'Have you got a key for this one?' he asked.

Colley tried a few keys from the bunch that the caretaker had given them earlier that evening, having been instructed in stern tones to tell no one what the detectives were doing. Having found the correct one, the sergeant slid open the drawer, which contained a selection of newspaper cuttings. Colley took out the top one, which was from the front page of an edition of the *Sheffield Star* published two years previously. He held it up so that Blizzard could read the headline.

*Notorious city gangster dies in prison*

Colley turned his attention to the opening sentence of the report.

'Infamous Sheffield gangster Edward Marsden died last night in his prison cell after suffering a massive heart attack,' he read. The sergeant looked at his boss. 'You heard of him?'

'Vaguely,' said Blizzard. 'Read on.'

'Seventy-one-year-old Marsden died at Full Sutton maximum security prison near York, where he has been held ever since he was found guilty of the murder of gangland rival Bobby Ross in 2004. Marsden, who headed up one of Sheffield's most notorious gangs in the 1990s and noughties, had always maintained his innocence, claiming that the evidence that led to him being found guilty after a two-week trial was fabricated by police. An internal inquiry subsequently exonerated the officers involved.'

Colley stopped reading and looked at his boss.

'Hey, didn't Alan start his career in South Yorkshire?' he said.

'He did, yes, but in Rotherham, not Sheffield.'

'Nevertheless, it's still a bit of a coincidence, isn't it? And as you are always telling me, you don't believe in coincidences in murder investigations. Blizzard's First Law, as I recall.'

'It is indeed,' said the inspector. 'Are the other cuttings about the same case?'

Colley flicked through them and nodded.

'They're all about Edward Marsden, yeah,' he said. 'Mostly about the trial. Maybe Sally is planning to make a documentary about the case. This may have nothing to do with Alan. I've never heard him mention this Marsden fellow. In fact, he never really said anything about his days in South Yorkshire.'

The sergeant stopped at another cutting from the *Sheffield Star*.

'Hey, this is interesting,' he said. 'It appeared a couple of days after the trial came to an end.'

He held the cutting up so that Blizzard could read the headline.

> *Special investigation – the police plot that sent gangster down*

'It's about Marsden's claims that police fabricated the evidence against him,' said the sergeant, quickly scanning the page. 'The newspaper quotes a police source as saying that the undercover officer lied in the witness box about hearing Marsden admit to killing Bobby Ross because he was told to do so by an unnamed senior officer.'

'Are they named?'

'No.'

Blizzard thought for a few moments.

'We need to find out more about this,' he said.

After leaving Colley to photocopy the newspaper cuttings, replace them in the drawer and return the keys to the caretaker, Blizzard headed home, dropping in to see Claire Steele on his way. She still looked pale but the inspector thought that she looked stronger. More composed. More in control. Maybe more able to answer difficult questions, he decided.

'How have you been?' asked Blizzard as they sat in the living room, her on the sofa, him in an armchair.

'It's been difficult,' she said.

'I'm sure,' said the inspector. 'And what about the kids? How have they taken it?'

'Evie's very upset,' said Claire. 'Archie's too young to fully understand everything but he knows that something has happened to his dad. I keep meaning to tell him that Alan is dead but somehow I can never find the words.'

Blizzard nodded. Ever since Mikey had been born, the inspector had found his priorities changing. The driven detective with an obsessive approach to the job had been gradually replaced by someone who was much more sympathetic to those officers with children. It was something he had tried to work into the way he ran his department. An oppressive silence had settled on the room. Blizzard felt an urge to banish it.

'Is your sister not staying with you?' he asked. 'You shouldn't really be on your own.'

'She had to go home,' said Claire. 'She's going to ring me later to check that I'm alright but I'm going to have to learn to cope sometime. Have you made any progress in your investigation? The newspaper said that you were following up several leads but it didn't say what they were.'

'Not to go outside these four walls…' said the inspector.

She nodded.

'But there may be a link with a gangster,' continued the inspector. 'An international gun-runner.'

'What would Alan have to do with a man like that?' asked Claire with surprise.

'It's possible that he and Sally Jackson were planning to make a documentary about him and that the gangster had Alan killed to stop it happening.'

'I told you that woman was involved somehow,' said Claire with venom. 'I've never trusted her. What's the name of this man? Is he from Hafton?'

'He's from Leeds. He's called Nathaniel Callaghan.'

'I've never heard of him,' said Claire.

'What about Edward Marsden?' asked Blizzard.

'Was he a gangster as well?'

'He was. From Sheffield and Alan used to work over that way, didn't he?'

'He was based in Rotherham,' said Claire. 'But he never really talked about his days with South Yorkshire Police and I've never heard him mention Edward Marsden. Why are you interested in him?'

'His name just cropped up.'

'I'm sorry but I can't help you.' Claire gave a sad smile. 'I seem to be saying that a lot, don't I? It's ironic really. I'm learning more about my husband now he's dead than I ever did when he was alive.'

Me, too, thought Blizzard, and I'm not liking any of it.

## Chapter twenty-five

The next morning, Blizzard was up early to feed Mikey his breakfast and catch up with events on the Island of Sodor. As he munched on toast and watched Toby the Tram Engine lose control on a steep hill and plough into a station at high speed, the inspector could not help wondering, as he often did, why the railway company had not had its licence to operate suspended and why The Fat Controller had not been arrested.

With breakfast completed, the inspector headed back to Abbey Road Police Station and was soon in his office, catching up on emails and other bureaucracy. Colley and Ramsey joined him just after 9am and took their seats at the desk. Ramsey, in particular, looked like a man with news to impart.

'I take it you have found out more about Edward Marsden?' said Blizzard.

'Sure have. I've just come off the phone from a mate of mine who used to work for South Yorkshire CID. He's long since retired but I rang him on the off-chance that he might know something. He says that, at the time of the murder, the gangs led by Edward Marsden and Bobby

Ross were competing for a share of the heroin market in Sheffield.'

'A lucrative trade,' said Blizzard.

'Indeed, and men had been murdered on both sides. On the night that Ross was killed, he had arranged to meet Marsden on a canal path so that they could thrash out their differences and come up with some kind of peace deal.'

'Just the two of them?' asked Blizzard.

'That was the agreement. Anyway, an hour later, a dog walker found Ross on the path, dead from a gunshot wound, and there was no sign of Marsden. He was arrested the next day.'

'Understandable,' said Blizzard. 'Motive and opportunity.'

'But no witnesses,' said Ramsey. 'And he denied it right from the moment that he was arrested. He said that he left the scene first and that Ross was alive. The cops had to release him without charge.'

'Have we found out anything about this alleged plot to fabricate evidence against him?' asked Blizzard.

'Yes, and this is where it gets murky,' said Ramsey. 'Very murky indeed. According to my mate, the DCI in charge of the case – a chap called Neil Sykes – was a somewhat shady character. He sent in an undercover officer to infiltrate Marsden's gang and a few weeks later, lo and behold, Marsden is arrested on the word of the undercover guy. He was never named publicly and he gave evidence behind a screen while sitting in a separate building.'

'What exactly did he say?' asked Blizzard.

'That he heard Marsden admit to the killing in a bar one night. It was a pretty circumstantial case without his testimony, and there were no other witnesses to the conversation, but the jury believed him and found Marsden guilty. Marsden always claimed that the undercover officer made it up at Sykes' behest but an internal inquiry cleared everyone involved of wrongdoing and his attempts to appeal against his conviction came to nothing.'

'Does your pal know the name of the undercover officer?' asked Blizzard.

'If he does, he isn't saying.'

'There must have been some people who knew who it was,' said Colley.

'There was plenty of speculation at the time but Neil Sykes refused to name him and he went to his grave five years ago, having always refused to talk about it.'

'But we're thinking that it might have been Alan, are we?' asked Colley.

'Apparently, his name was one of several mentioned at the time,' said Ramsey. 'But only because he had been off work for several weeks. He explained his absence by saying that he was on a training course and folks decided that it could not be him because not even Neil Sykes would send a rookie into a situation that dangerous. However, he *was* based in South Yorkshire when the killing happened and he *did* leave the area soon after.'

Ramsey's mobile rang.

'Maybe this is a man who can tell us more,' he said. 'My pal said he'd ask Neil Sykes' oppo from the time if he would speak to us.'

* * *

That afternoon found Blizzard and Colley seated at a corner table in a motorway services café near Sheffield. Sitting opposite them was a thin-faced man with a wrinkled brow, whose thinning hair was streaked with grey. In between nervous glances around him, retired South Yorkshire Police Detective Sergeant Michael Quigley surveyed the Hafton officers with an uneasy expression on his face.

'I want you to know that I am here under sufferance,' he said, looking at Blizzard. 'I only agreed to meet you because your DI Ramsey said you were the type of man who would charge me with obstruction if I refused to help.'

'We appreciate you agreeing to see us,' said Blizzard. 'And Chris Ramsey is right. This *is* a murder inquiry, after all.'

'Well, none of this is on the record,' said Quigley. He reached for his cup of coffee. 'I have to be careful what I say.'

'Why?' asked Blizzard. 'Neil Sykes and Edward Marsden are both dead, aren't they? And I doubt anyone will be that interested in taking action against you.'

'That's not what worries me. You're investigating the death of Alan Steele, aren't you?'

'Yes. He was one of my team.'

'Then you can see why I'm being careful,' said Quigley. 'If someone had a grudge against him, they could have one against me as well. I don't want to end up like him.'

'Are we right in assuming that he was the undercover officer who gave evidence against Marsden?' asked Colley.

'Keep your voice down,' hissed Quigley. He looked nervously round the largely deserted café again. 'You never know who's listening.'

Satisfied that they no one was taking any notice of them, he relaxed slightly.

'OK,' he said. 'Yes, he was.'

'How did he get mixed up with all this?' asked Blizzard.

'It was Neil's idea.' Quigley took a sip of coffee. 'When it became clear that we could not prove that Marsden shot Bobby Ross, he said we should send in an undercover officer.'

'How come he chose Alan?' asked Colley.

'He was an ambitious young bobby and Neil told him that working undercover would be good for his career, that it might fast-track him into CID, which is where Alan wanted to be. The main reason Neil picked him was that no one knew him in Sheffield. I told Neil that it was not a good idea – the kid was too green and he'd had no training in working undercover – but he ignored me. To be fair to Neil, Alan seemed really keen to do it.'

'Did Neil send him in with instructions to make up evidence?' asked Colley.

'I don't think so. I think that he genuinely hoped that Alan would turn something up but when he didn't, Neil decided to try something else. What you've got to remember is that he started his career at a time when some officers thought nothing of fitting up suspects. It was a way of life for someone like Neil Sykes.'

'How come he got Alan to play along with it?' asked Blizzard. 'He was always straight during his time with us.'

'The kid was in way over his head,' said Quigley. 'Terrified that he'd be unmasked and end up like Bobby Ross. He'd have done anything to get out of there so when Neil suggested he make something up, he saw his chance.'

'Did anyone suspect he was the undercover officer?' asked Colley.

'His was one of a few names bandied about at the time but I don't think anyone seriously thought it was him,' said Quigley. 'The favourite was a detective from Doncaster but only me and Neil knew who it really was and neither of us ever said anything.'

'And no one ever threatened Alan at the time?' asked Blizzard.

'Not that I know of, and he transferred to your neck of the woods a few weeks after Marsden was arrested anyway. I lost track of him after the trial. The next time I saw him was when he turned up on that television programme.'

'Do you think one of Marsden's old gang recognised him?' asked Colley.

'I doubt it,' said Quigley. 'I only saw him once when he was undercover and I don't think his mother would have recognised him. He had a beard and let his hair grow long. Nothing like the clean-shaven guy on the television. Besides, after Marsden was sent to prison, the gang broke apart. Several of them are dead now and I can't see any of the others wanting to kill Alan after all these years. What would they have to gain?'

'Well, someone cared enough to kill him,' said Blizzard.

'But who?' asked Quigley. 'And why now?'

Blizzard thought of Sally Jackson.

'Did Marsden have any family?' he asked. 'A daughter maybe?'

Quigley looked surprised.

'How do you know that?' he said.

'I take it the answer is yes, then?' said Blizzard.

'It was tragic,' said Quigley. 'Marsden's wife killed herself six months after he was jailed – she was always a bit unstable and him going to prison tipped her over the edge. Cut her wrists and bled to death in the bath. The kid was sent into care.'

'What was her name?' asked Blizzard.

Quigley thought for a few moments, trying to summon the memory.

'Hannah, I think,' he said. 'I don't know what happened to her after she went into care.'

'I have this awful feeling that it wasn't good,' said Blizzard. He looked at Colley. 'Motive and opportunity.'

Colley nodded.

'And nigh on twenty years to let it fester,' he said.

# Chapter twenty-six

Blizzard and Colley returned to Abbey Road Police Station shortly after 5pm and the moment they arrived, the inspector headed for Chris Ramsey's office. Ramsey had just come off the desk phone when Blizzard entered.

'It's her alright,' said Ramsey, his eyes gleaming.

'Are you sure?' said Blizzard, sitting down.

'That was the fostering people in Sheffield,' said Ramsey, nodding at the phone. 'It took a bit of persuasion to get them to talk to me but, when they did, they confirmed that Hannah Marsden was fostered not long after her mother died and that her name was changed to Sally Jackson.'

'Why?' asked Blizzard.

'Apparently, the foster parents thought that a break with the past was in the kid's interest, that being known as the daughter of a notorious gangster was not helpful. She would seem to have had an appalling childhood, shunted from one set of foster parents to the next, and abused by the last ones. There was a police investigation but it came to nothing. The poor kid was failed by everyone who dealt with her.' Ramsey shook his head. 'No wonder she was so angry at Alan. Without his lies, there's every chance that she would have had a normal childhood.'

'Do we know when she found out who she really is?' asked Blizzard.

'She approached the fostering people earlier this year because she wanted to find out the identity of her real parents. Given that both of them were dead, they didn't see any harm in telling her. Presumably, she found out the rest from the newspaper cuttings.'

'But who told her where Alan fits into the story?' asked Blizzard.

'That I don't know, but one thing seems certain. When she did find out about him, it was like lighting the blue touch paper. My guess is that behind the professional façade, Sally Jackson aka Hannah Marsden, is a seething mass of hatred and resentment.'

Blizzard shook his head.

'What a mess,' he said.

'So what do we do now?' asked Ramsey.

'Arrest her. I want her out of circulation asap, especially if she's still got the gun.' Blizzard glanced at the wall clock, stood up and headed for door. 'She's usually in her office at this time of day. Come on.'

'Shouldn't we call in the firearms team?' said Ramsey.

'As far as we are aware, she doesn't know that we're onto her,' said Blizzard. 'If we call in Firearms, it could go pear-shaped, whereas if we wander in we can catch her off-guard.'

'You hope,' said Ramsey.

Reluctantly, he followed his boss into the corridor and the two detectives tentatively approached the television company's office. The room was deserted and in darkness and Ramsey could not help feel a sense of relief, not that he allowed his boss to see it.

'What now?' he asked.

'We put the word out for her. Including ports and airports,' said Blizzard. 'And we bring Ray Varone in.

There's a good chance that he's more involved in Alan's murder than we thought. I think he gave Hannah the gun.'

He was about to elaborate on the comment when his mobile rang. He took the call. 'Wendy, what can I do for you?'

'Thought you'd like to know that one of our surveillance teams spotted your television producer in a park in Leeds. She was meeting Ray Varone again.'

'Is she still there?' said Blizzard urgently.

'We assume that she's on her way back to Hafton. She left an hour ago. Is there a problem?'

'We need to talk to her again. And Ray as well.'

'Why do you–?' began Talbot.

'I'll tell you later,' said the inspector.

'Can't you tell–?'

'No.'

'Don't you trust me?' said Talbot. She sounded offended. 'He doesn't trust me, Matt.'

The detectives heard Riley mutter something in the background but could not make out what he had said.

'That's the problem with MI5 being involved,' said Talbot. 'They've got everyone looking suspiciously at each other.'

'Well, someone is leaking information,' said Blizzard pointedly.

'Yes, well, it's not me or Matt,' came Talbot's icy reply. 'And the reason I ask is that I am trying to work out if you really need to see Ray Varone at this particular moment because we're closing in on the Moroccan gang and they are already getting nervous with what's going on. If they hear that you've been talking to Ray again, it could bring the whole lot crashing down. Can't you tell me *anything*?'

'Sorry, Wendy,' said Blizzard. 'Maybe later.'

'If that's the way you want it…' said Talbot and ended the call abruptly.

Blizzard noticed that Ramsey was looking at him keenly.

'I thought you trusted Wendy,' said the detective inspector.

Before Ramsey could question his boss further, Blizzard was striding down the corridor. Within the hour, he and Colley were heading west to Leeds again, leaving Chris Ramsey at Abbey Road Police Station to co-ordinate the search for Sally Jackson. On arrival in the city, the Hafton detectives met up with James Rowles, went through the usual ritual of the briefing with the firearms team, then headed out to Varone's home once more. Sitting in the back seat, Rowles was quiet as Blizzard guided the vehicle through darkened streets, following a minibus and a marked patrol car.

'You OK?' asked Blizzard, glancing over his shoulder.

'Like I said, we had hoped to keep Varone on the outside for a little longer,' replied Rowles. 'And you haven't told me why you want to see him again. I understand that you wouldn't tell Wendy either. Why so secretive all of a sudden?'

Blizzard did not reply and before Rowles could question him further, they had arrived at Varone's house. Rowles cursed when he saw that, as with the previous raid, the lights were on in the house.

'This is nothing to do with me,' he said quickly. 'I didn't tell him.'

'Well, someone did,' said Blizzard.

The inspector got out of the car and strode towards the house, followed by Colley. As with their previous visit, the front door swung open to reveal Ray Varone standing in the hallway, fully dressed and with his arms crossed in a defiant posture. He looked at Rowles.

'How come you are letting them get away with this, James?' he said. 'This is beginning to look like harassment.'

'I told you before, it's not my show,' said Rowles. He glanced at Blizzard. 'Ask him.'

'Well?' demanded Varone. He glowered at Blizzard. 'What do you want?'

'First off, who told you we were coming?' asked Blizzard.

Varone shook his head. He had the air of a man who believed that he was in control of the situation.

'You don't need to know,' he said. 'But if you're here because you want me to give a statement about Nathaniel ordering the murder, I told you last time that it ain't going to happen.'

Blizzard gave a slight smile; his tactic of keeping secret the exact reason for the visit was working, the element of surprise was his. He took a step towards the gangster.

'Ray Varone,' he said. 'You are under arrest on suspicion of conspiracy to murder Alan Steele.'

Rowles looked at the inspector in surprise and Varone still looked stunned as Colley led him from the house and out to the waiting vehicles.

## Chapter twenty-seven

An hour later, the Hafton detectives were sitting in an interview room at a local police station and staring across the desk at Ray Varone. Despite his attempts to present a relaxed demeanour, there was an uneasiness about the gangster and he could not stop the beads of sweat glistening on his brow. Blizzard gave a thin smile; he sensed that for the first time in the inquiry they were gaining the upper hand. The fact that the prisoner had declined the services of the solicitor Gerald Crabtree only served to strengthen the inspector's belief that Nathaniel Callaghan knew nothing of Varone's double-dealing ways and that the gangster was anxious that things stayed that way.

'You're making a big mistake,' said Varone. He was recovering some of his self-confidence. 'I told you that your bloke's death is down to Nathaniel. I had nothing to do with it.'

'We know about Hannah Marsden,' said Blizzard.

The comment had the desired effect and Varone stared at him in amazement. Blizzard gave another smile; the revelation had wrong-footed the gangster and his confidence was crumbling.

'Who's she?' asked Varone, trying to sound as if he genuinely had no idea.

'You know exactly who she is,' said the inspector. 'So, tell me what you know. Did she approach you or did you approach her?'

'I don't know what you–'

'Don't play games with us!' snapped Blizzard. 'When did you find out Sally Jackson's real identity?'

Varone did not reply.

'It's in your interest to tell us,' said Blizzard. 'Because if you don't, I'll have to ask Nathaniel if he knows and that could mean that I might accidentally let slip that you tried to frame him for Alan's murder.'

'You wouldn't dare,' said Varone.

'Try me,' replied Blizzard. 'Look, Ray, we know that Hannah shot Alan Steele. What we need to find out is who's idea it was. Yours or hers?'

Varone thought for a few moments.

'I seem to be trapped between you and Nathaniel,' he said eventually with a rueful grin. 'It's not exactly a pleasant place to be. Can we do a deal? I tell you what I know about Hannah and you give me enough time to get out of the country before Nathaniel finds out what's been happening?'

'No deals,' said Blizzard. 'But tell me what you know and I might change my mind. Whose idea was it to kill Alan?'

'Hannah's,' said Varone. 'We'd had several phone conversations about the documentary and I kept telling her that there was no way Nathaniel would agree to it then, out of the blue, she announced that she was Edward Marsden's daughter. Tried to make out that it made her some kind of expert on organised crime, which was why we could trust her to make the film.'

'And you said?' asked Blizzard.

'I still said no and I didn't hear anything from her for several weeks. I thought she'd given up then she rang me one evening. She was really upset. She said that the police officer who worked with her on the television show had got drunk the previous night and told that he had once lied to have a major league criminal sent down. Hannah realised that he was talking about her father and that he was the man she blamed for her mother's death. She asked me if I would help her to murder him.'

'And you said yes?' asked Blizzard.

'Not at first. I didn't think she was serious and, even if she was, I wanted nothing to do with her crazy idea. She's unhinged.'

'So what changed your mind?'

'Nathaniel,' said Varone. 'I suppose you know about the deal with the Moroccans?'

Blizzard nodded.

'Well, he refused to listen when I told him how dangerous they are,' said Varone. 'I had to do something to distract him while I got them off our backs.'

'And you saw an opportunity to frame him for the murder?' said the inspector.

'I knew that you'd never get the charge to stick but I reckoned that it would give me enough time to sort things out. Hannah told Alan about the documentary and fixed up a meet in Leeds. I didn't realise we were being watched. I thought we'd found somewhere out of sight.'

'And Gary Race?' asked Colley. 'Where does he fit into it?'

'He doesn't. I got hold of a car like his and put fake plates on then drove it to Hafton. Everyone knows that he's a loyal Nathaniel Callaghan man.'

'And the van driver who said he'd seen the car?' asked Blizzard.

'All part of the set-up. I paid him to make himself scarce after he'd talked to you.'

'And you gave Hannah the Murder Gun?' said Blizzard.

'Yeah. I'd been looking after it for years.'

'How did you explain its reappearance to Nathaniel?' asked Colley.

'I told him that I had been burgled and that they had broken into the safe where I kept it.'

'And he believed you?' said the sergeant.

'If he didn't, he didn't say anything. He's always trusted me, has Nathaniel. I was pretty sure that he would not suspect me of double-crossing him.'

'And Hannah shot Alan?' asked Blizzard.

Varone nodded.

'She told Alan that we'd changed our mind about doing the documentary and that I wanted another meet and that I was coming to Hafton,' he said. 'Hannah met him in the car park by the river and took him to the warehouse. The rest you know and, if you ask me, he deserved everything he got.'

'Were you there when he was shot?' asked Colley. The sergeant was struggling to control his revulsion at the cold-blooded nature of what he was being told.

'No, I made sure that the car had been spotted by the cameras on the dual carriageway, parked up for a while then headed back towards Leeds. Hannah rang me later to say that he was dead.'

Colley was silent and Blizzard noted that his colleague was struggling to retain control of his emotions so he asked the next question.

'How did she sound when she rang you?' he asked.

'Calm,' said Varone. 'Very calm. Like a pro. Fair chilled the blood, it did. She's one dangerous lady, is Hannah Marsden.'

'And where is the gun now?' asked the inspector.

'She hasn't given it back to me yet. We were going to let the dust settle before we did the handover.'

Blizzard and Colley exchanged worried glances.

'So she's still got it?' said the inspector.

'Sure has,' said Varone.

He gave a wicked smile, held up his hand to make the shape of a firearm and used his thumb to replicate someone pulling a trigger.

'So you'd better watch yourselves,' he said. 'Who knows what she might do next?'

# Chapter twenty-eight

Having arranged for Varone to be transported to Hafton, Blizzard and Colley started on their own journey back to the city. They had been on the motorway for half an hour and were approaching the turn-off for a services complex when Blizzard flicked on the car's indicator.

'Fancy a cuppa?' he asked.

The sergeant looked at his boss in surprise.

'Don't you want to get back to Hafton?' he said.

'Not yet,' said Blizzard, getting out of the car. 'I promised to buy Wendy Talbot a cup of tea first.'

'Wendy Talbot?' said Colley, following his boss across the car park. 'I would have thought you were the last person that she wanted to see. According to Chris, you all but accused her of leaking information to Callaghan.'

Blizzard said nothing as he led the way into the services and they headed for the coffee shop. Talbot was sitting at a table in the far corner of the room and next to her was MI5 officer Jane Kenworthy. A teapot for two sat in front of them next to an opened packet of biscuits.

'What's she doing here?' said the sergeant, unable to hide his irritation. He looked at Blizzard. 'What's happening?'

'Who says I can't play politics?' replied Blizzard cheerfully. He led the way to the table and gestured to the teapot. 'Ladies, what a pleasant surprise. Top-up?'

With the drinks purchased and everyone sitting round the table, Kenworthy passed the packet of biscuits to Colley.

'Hobnob?' she said.

'Would someone like to explain what the hell is going on?' asked Colley. 'I thought that everyone was supposed to be at everyone else's throat?'

'That's what we want people to think,' said Talbot. 'We can't have them thinking that we're all working together, can we now?'

'However, we are,' said Blizzard. 'Ever since the farce when the MI5 guys followed us to Hafton, we have been working to track down the cop who's been leaking information. Actually, it was Arthur's idea.'

'Could you not trust me?' asked Colley. He was unable to hide the disappointment in his voice.

'I'm sorry, David,' said Blizzard. He reached out to touch the sergeant gently on the arm. 'I knew it wasn't you that was passing on information but we decided that we couldn't afford to make any exceptions until we knew who it was. One wrong word to the wrong person and it would all be for nothing.'

'I guess that makes sense,' said Colley. He seemed happier once he had received the explanation.

'Besides,' said Talbot with a hint of sadness in her voice, 'it turns out that not all of us can rely on the services of such a reliable right-hand man as John here.'

She glanced at Kenworthy, who reached into her bag and produced several sheets of bank transactions, which she slid across the desk for the sergeant to look at. Colley read the name on top of the first sheet and gave them a bewildered look.

'Who's Mark Paterson?' he asked.

'Mark Paterson is the name that Matt Riley uses on a bank account we were not supposed to find,' said Kenworthy. 'It took a lot of work to track it down, I can tell you.'

Colley's eyes widened.

'Matt Riley?' he said. 'Are you sure? I would never have suspected him. I thought it might be James Rowles.'

'We had him on our shortlist as well,' said Kenworthy. 'Until we discovered Matt's weakness for online poker. As you can see from the bank account, he's been running up some big debts.'

'So I see,' said Colley, studying the figures. 'I take it the incoming payments are from Nathaniel Callaghan?'

'And Varone,' said Talbot. 'He's been selling information to both of them. I am afraid that he's been playing everyone off against each other.'

'We couldn't let him think that we were onto him,' said Blizzard. 'So we hatched a little plan. That's why myself and Wendy staged our fallout. The result was that Matt knew that we planned to bring Varone in but he did not know that we had worked out Sally Jackson's real identity. You saw how Varone reacted when we turned up, David. That was enough to confirm our suspicions.'

Colley shook his head in disbelief.

'So what happens now?' he asked. 'Are you going to arrest him?'

'All in good time,' said Talbot. 'He's more use to us doing his thing rather than being locked up. Varone's out of the picture now, and John's going to make sure that it stays that way, but we're keen to keep a connection with Callaghan. And we need that, because the word is that the handover of the weapons to the Moroccans will happen sometime over the next couple of days and that they are going to bring them through Hafton Docks.'

'Hafton?' said the inspector in surprise. 'I thought the truck was coming in through Immingham?'

'According to our informant in Morocco, all the activity around Callaghan and Varone has spooked the North Africans to such an extent that they have changed their plans,' said Talbot. 'Immingham is now a decoy and they have a man on the inside at Hafton who will wave the truck through. Matt does not know that we know about the decoy so we hope that he will tell Callaghan that we're on the wrong track. I've even told him to go over to Immingham and handle things for us.'

'And where is the real handover going to take place?' asked Blizzard.

'Not sure yet,' said Talbot. 'But wherever it is, we'll be there and the word is that, with Varone gone, Nathaniel may be forced to break the habit of a lifetime and handle the handover himself. He won't be expecting us to turn up so we could finally nick him for something.'

'Ray said he was starting to make mistakes,' said Blizzard. His eyes gleamed. 'What was it that Hannibal Smith used to say? I love it when a plan comes together?'

# Chapter twenty-nine

On the detectives' arrival back at Abbey Road Police Station, Blizzard and Colley headed for the CID squad room where the inspector caught up with developments with his team.

'Has Varone arrived?' asked Blizzard.

'He's been booked in and taken to a cell ready for you to interview him,' said Ramsey. 'For a man with his reputation, he looks stunned at what has happened to him.'

'Yeah,' said Blizzard. 'It wasn't part of his plan. Any word on Hannah Marsden?'

'Not yet,' said Ramsey. 'We've checked all the places that we know she goes but there's been no sign of her, and her colleagues say that she has not been in at work all day and is not answering her mobile. We've had the chopper up most of the day but they've not seen anything. Looks like she's worked out that we're onto her.'

'Maybe she's left the city,' said Colley.

'If she has, she wasn't in her car,' said Ramsey. 'It's been parked outside her house all day.'

'Well, she's out there somewhere,' said Blizzard. He glanced towards the window; it was almost dusk. 'And call it instinct, but I don't think she's that far away.'

He looked at Ramsey.

'Did you sort out that armed guard for Claire?' he asked.

'I did, yeah. It took a bit of persuasion but she's stayed in all day and kept the kids off school.'

'How is she?' asked Blizzard.

'She muttered something about always knowing that "that woman" was bad news,' said Ramsey.

'I'll bet she did,' replied Blizzard with a slight smile. He stood up. 'Keep me posted, will you?'

'Sure,' said Ramsey. 'Where will you be?'

'I'm going to update Arthur, then I'll go and see Varone.'

* * *

It was a pensive inspector who walked along the corridor to see the superintendent.

'Ah, just the man,' said Ronald as his old friend walked into his office and sat down. 'I've just had Miranda from the CPS on the phone, looking for you. She says that you are fine to charge Ray Varone with conspiracy to commit murder.'

'Excellent,' said Blizzard. 'Anything else I need to know about?'

'Yes, there's a limit to how long we can keep the media in the dark about what's happening. The press office is being given a hard time and we can't keep telling the journalists that we are responding to a vague report of someone with a gun. We may need to give more details.'

'Can't we issue a press release?'

'It may need more than that,' said the superintendent. 'The control room is receiving increasing numbers of calls from worried members of the public and you can imagine how wild the speculation on social media has been. I am afraid that if we keep saying nothing, there'll be even more panic as darkness falls. I think we may have to hold a press conference tonight to offer some reassurance.'

'And how exactly do you think I should do that?' asked the inspector. 'Don't worry, folks, it's only a madwoman with a gun who is hell-bent on revenge.'

Ronald gave a slight smile.

'I'm sure you'll find the words,' he said.

'Your faith in my eloquence is heart-warming,' said Blizzard and stood up.

'When do you want to hold the press conference?' asked Ronald.

'Can you give me an hour? I need to get Varone charged first – we'll interview him in the morning – and I think I owe it to Claire to go and update her on what's happening.'

'Good idea,' said Ronald. 'An hour it is.'

* * *

Five minutes later, Blizzard was standing with Ray Varone in the custody suite. The gangster still looked bewildered at what was happening to him.

'Are you sure we can't do a deal?' he asked plaintively.

'You've got nothing we want,' said Blizzard. 'And it won't be long before we have Nathaniel as well. The game's up, Ray.'

Varone gave the inspector a sick look but did not reply.

Ten minutes later, with his prisoner having been charged and returned to his cell, the inspector was back in the squad room.

'Sarah,' he said, walking over to Allatt's desk. 'I'm going to see Claire to update her on what's been happening. You OK to go with me?'

'Sure,' said the detective constable, reaching for her coat.

Together, they headed for the back door, which led into the yard behind the station. Having pushed open the door and emerged into the chill night air, they headed for the inspector's car. As they did so, a movement caught Blizzard's eye, something lurking in the shadows. Instinct told him immediately that they were in danger and his body stiffened.

'What's wrong?' asked Allatt, alarmed at his sudden reaction.

'I'm not sure,' said Blizzard. He peered again into the shadows in the far corner of the yard. 'Anyone there?'

Hannah Marsden emerged from the darkness and stood pointing a gun at him. Blizzard tried to stay calm but was acutely aware of the pounding of his heart and the beads of sweat forming on his brow. Standing behind him, Sarah Allatt froze and stared at her in horror.

'Oh, God,' she whispered.

'Stay calm,' said the inspector in a low voice.

He looked at Hannah.

'Now don't do anything silly, Hannah,' he said.

He was relieved that his voice was steady and did not betray the fear that was coursing through his body. He knew that he had to take control of the situation but in a way that ensured that she did not panic and pull the trigger accidentally. Her next words did little to calm his nerves.

'Who says it would be silly?' she said. Her voice sounded strange, distant, detached. 'I mean, what have I got to lose? Ray told me that you would come for me one day and I know that you searched my office so I must assume you found the newspaper cuttings. Is Ray here?'

'He is, yes.'

'Under arrest?'

'Yes. We've charged him with conspiracy to commit murder.'

'It wasn't his idea, you know,' she said.

'I know but he helped you.'

She considered the comment for a few moments then nodded as if accepting the CPS decision. Having slightly lowered the gun, she lifted it back up again to point at the inspector. Blizzard noted with alarm that her hand was shaking. Despite his precarious situation, the inspector found himself staring at the gun with morbid fascination and thinking of all the men that had done the same thing in their final moments. They must have felt the way that he was feeling before they died, he thought; must have stared at the legendary weapon and wondered if theirs was the name on the bullet.

Blizzard had heard people who had been in similar situations later recount how their life had flashed before them. The inspector, who had faced weapons several times in his career, did not recall the showreel of his life playing when it happened but he did remember how time had stood still, as it did now. Rebuking himself for allowing his mind to wander, and marvelling at the fact that such a thing was possible at such a time of peril, Blizzard dragged himself back to the here and now and realised that Hannah was speaking.

'Don't think I won't kill you,' she said. 'I thought nothing of killing that lying bastard pal of yours and I'll think nothing of killing you. In fact, it'll be a pleasure.'

'Look, I know that Alan hurt you–' began Blizzard.

'You know? You know nothing!' Her words were spat out with venom. 'You cannot even begin to understand the damage that he did.'

'So tell me,' said Blizzard, acutely aware that he was talking to save his life and desperately trying to buy time. 'But put the gun down first. We can't talk with you pointing it at me.'

She did not lower the weapon.

'Do you know how my mother died?' she said in a voice laced with bitterness. 'Do you?'

'I know that she comm–'

'She filled herself with whisky and got into the bath where she slit her wrists with a knife,' said Hannah. Her voice was trembling now as emotion overwhelmed her. 'Then she lay there and drowned in her own blood. Can you imagine what that was like? To lie there and slowly die, knowing that your child is asleep in the next room?'

Tears glistened in Marsden's eyes and the hand holding the gun started to shake. Blizzard let her gather her thoughts and said nothing. There did not seem to be the words, anyway.

'Alan Steele deserved everything he got,' said Hannah. 'Do you know that he begged for his life? Did you know that, Chief Inspector? When he was down on his knees, he begged me to spare him through his tears. Begged me to spare his wretched life for the sake of his children.'

She gave a mirthless laugh.

'Can you imagine that?' she said. 'For the sake of his children! Well, he didn't think about me when he told his lies, did he? Do you know how difficult it was to control myself as he told me what he had done? Do you?' Her voice almost became a scream. 'Well, do you?'

'I don't, I never can,' said Blizzard. He felt sick as he waited for her to squeeze the trigger. He tried to remain calm, to rationalise with her, even though he sensed that she had moved far beyond that point. 'I can't imagine what you went through, but put the gun down and we can…'

His voiced tailed off as a wicked look crossed her face, her eyes glinting as she gestured for him to get down onto his knees.

'Are you going to beg for your life, Chief Inspector?' she said. 'Are you going to beg for the sake of your beloved Mikey?'

Blizzard felt a tug of emotion at the thought of his son sitting in his highchair, eating yoghurt and kiwi fruit while watching *Thomas the Tank Engine*. Tears glistened in the inspector's eyes but with an immense effort, he suppressed the emotion and shook his head.

'I'm not going to beg,' he said. He was relieved that his voice was still steady. 'Not for you or anyone.'

The inspector caught sight of movement behind Hannah as a firearms officer, part of the team that been patrolling the area all day, emerged from the shadows and advanced slowly with his weapon trained on Hannah. She noticed the inspector's change of focus, realised immediately what he had seen, and whirled round with a cry of animal rage. But she was too late and a shot rang out, the bullet slamming into her chest and forcing her to her knees with a shocked gasp. And there she remained, motionless, silent, eyes still open, in the position that she had forced her final victim to adopt before he met his death.

Blizzard gave a cry of relief and Sarah Allatt stared in shocked silence at the dead woman. After he had regained his composure, Blizzard looked at the young constable, whose face was drained of colour and whose legs were no longer capable of holding her weight as she slumped against the wall.

'Are you OK?' he said.

She nodded but did not speak. As the door to the station opened and officers poured into the yard, Blizzard looked at the firearms officer.

'I had no option but to shoot,' said the officer.

'You'll get no argument from me,' said Blizzard.

As colleagues gathered round the two detectives, one of the other firearms officers opened up the Murder Gun and removed a bullet. He walked over to Blizzard and held it up so that he could clearly see the initials etched in it. *J B*. The inspector looked at Colley.

'I think I'd like to go home and see Mikey,' he said. 'Maybe even catch bath-time.'

# Chapter thirty

The following day, shortly after 7pm, the truck rumbled down the ferry ramp and onto Hafton Docks, where it was waved through as predicted before heading towards the city centre. The driver showed little sign he had noticed that he was being tailed by a car driven by John Blizzard and carrying Wendy Talbot and David Colley. The detectives were part of a large surveillance team and the cars continually switched positions to avoid alerting the truck driver that he was being followed as he guided his vehicle onto the western bypass. As Blizzard's car approached the Tesco supermarket, he pointed to the row of derelict warehouses on the roadside.

'That's where Alan was killed,' he said.

Talbot shook her head.

'A tragic business,' she said. 'I hear that Ray Varone was remanded in custody this morning?'

'Yeah. He's back before the magistrates early next week and the CPS reckon the trial will be in eight months.'

'Will he plead guilty?' asked Talbot.

'The CPS seem to think so,' said Blizzard.

* * *

Five minutes later, the truck left the city, still heading west on the dual carriageway. The radio in Blizzard's car crackled into life. It was the head of the Hafton firearms team, travelling in one of the vehicles behind Blizzard's car.

'Any word on the location for the handover yet?' he asked.

'Sorry, nothing yet,' said the inspector. 'My money's on the old aerodrome outside Canderby.'

'Makes sense,' said the firearms officer. 'It's well away from the houses.'

Blizzard was proved right and, ten minutes later, the truck pulled off the dual carriageway and onto the slip road that took it along the main street that snaked its way through the picturesque village of Canderby. Once the truck had emerged from the other side of the village, it slowed and turned off onto the deserted aerodrome site, finally coming to a halt and cutting its lights. Blizzard brought his vehicle to a halt on the road, having turned off his own headlights. Within a minute, the two cars containing the firearms officers drew to a halt behind him.

Talbot peered into the darkness, only able to make out the truck because of the dim light filtering from the cab. Seconds lengthened into minutes, minutes into half an hour and half an hour into a hour and still nothing happened.

'What's he waiting for?' murmured Talbot. 'Where are the Moroccans?'

On hour became two and still there was no movement on the road leading to the aerodrome. Talbot's mobile phone rang and she glanced at the screen.

'Matt in Immingham,' she said. She took the call. 'Matt, what's happening?'

'Nothing.'

'What do you mean nothing?'

'Just that,' said Riley. 'I've just been to check and the truck we were tipped off about was not on the ferry. I reckon we've been conned. The truck must be coming in somewhere else. What do you want me to do?'

'Give it another half hour then we'll call it a day,' said Talbot. She ended the call and frowned. 'I think that we've all been played for fools.'

Blizzard nodded.

'So do I,' he said. The inspector reached for his radio. 'It's OK for the firearms team to go in. It looks like it's a blowout.'

The two vehicles carrying the firearms officers entered the aerodrome at speed and came to a halt twenty metres from the truck. The officers disembarked and ran towards the lorry, one of them shouting a warning as he wrenched open the driver's door.

'Get out of the cab!' shouted the officer, pointing his weapon at the driver.

The truck driver, who did not appear to be surprised by what was happening, did as he was told. Other firearms officers checked the remainder of the vehicle, two of them pulling open the rear doors, their torches revealing that the truck was empty. The lead officer turned to watch the detectives as they approached across the car park.

'You're free to take a look,' he said. 'But I don't think you're going to like it.'

Wendy Talbot peered into the empty wagon and cursed. Blizzard gave a slight smile.

'Something tells me that Nathaniel Callaghan is not as senile as Ray Varone thinks he is,' he said.

* * *

Over at Immingham Docks, Jane Kenworthy and a fellow MI5 officer approached Matt Riley's vehicle and knocked on the window, startling the detective. The game was up.

## Chapter thirty-one

The next morning, Blizzard took Wendy Talbot over to Leeds where they met up once more with James Rowles and all three made their way to the office block owned by Nathaniel Callaghan, having this time opted to dispense with the support of the firearms unit. Sitting in the back seat of the inspector's car, James Rowles was quiet on the journey.

'You OK?' asked Blizzard.

'Yeah,' replied Rowles. 'It's just that I never thought I would see the day that Nathaniel Callaghan was arrested. I still can't believe that we'll make it stick.'

'We'll make it stick' said Talbot. 'Matt has promised to tell MI5 everything he knows.'

'Will it help him get a lighter sentence, do you think?' asked Rowles.

'I'm not sure,' said Talbot. 'The file that went to the CPS said how helpful he had been, so I suppose he might end up with a suspended sentence but it's far from certain. He's gone against everything the police stand for and a judge is likely to want to make an example of him as a warning to any other officer who might be tempted to cross the line.'

Rowles shook his head.

'I still don't understand why he did it,' he said.

'When money talks, people listen,' said Blizzard. He turned off the main road and onto the industrial estate. 'And it can be very persuasive.'

Silence settled on the car as the office block came into view. Blizzard turned into the car park and cut the engine and the three officers walked over to the front entrance. Blizzard rang the bell and, after a couple of minutes in which the inspector pressed the bell three more times, the shaven-headed man whom Blizzard and Colley had encountered on their previous visit opened the door and gave the detectives a surly look.

'What do you want?' he asked.

'To see Nathaniel,' said Blizzard.

'He ain't seeing anyone today,' said the man.

He tried to close the door but Blizzard gave it a hefty shove and the man stumbled backwards and dropped to one knee, temporarily winded. As the detectives strode past him, he got back to his feet and tried to block their way again but, this time, Blizzard snapped out a fist, which caught him in the mouth. Blood spurted from the man's lip and he glared at the inspector and raised his hand to strike back.

'Unless you want to get yourself arrested, I'd think very carefully about what you do next,' growled Blizzard. 'Because I really am not in the mood to be mucked about.'

'And neither am I,' said Rowles, stepping forward to stand next to the inspector.

The shaven-headed man hesitated then shrugged and stood aside.

'Good boy,' said Blizzard.

Talbot gave the inspector a questioning look.

'It's not like you to do something like that,' she said. 'I don't think I've ever seen you hit anyone.'

'You complaining?' asked Blizzard as the detectives climbed the stairs.

Talbot shook her head.

'Not me,' she said.

The officers entered the reception area and Callaghan's secretary stood up from her desk and opened her mouth to protest at the intrusion but thought twice about it as she saw the resolute expression on their faces. She sat down again. Blizzard gave her a smile.

'All we need is ten minutes,' said the inspector, referencing their previous meeting. 'Actually, come to think of it, it won't be that long.'

Cynthia gave him a baleful look but did not reply and the detectives walked into Callaghan's office without knocking. The gangster was sitting behind his desk and if he was surprised at their arrival, he was covering it well.

'Three of His Majesty's finest,' he said. 'I wonder what on earth could a humble import and export man such as myself could have done to warrant such attention. And after your brave actions in stopping an empty lorry, too! Did your people have a nice time at Immingham, Miss Talbot?'

'I take it that the firearms came in through another port?' said Talbot.

'And what firearms would they be?' asked Callaghan, feigning innocence. 'I don't know about any firearms.'

The gangster seemed to be enjoying himself, exuding confidence despite the stern demeanour of his visitors. Contrary to the picture that Ray Varone had painted of him, Nathaniel Callaghan was not a man whose grip was loosening. He was a man in control. Blizzard allowed himself a thin smile, anticipating what was to come. He would relish it.

'We think that you *do* know about the guns,' said Talbot.

'I take it that you have been listening to Ray Varone's fanciful stories about Moroccan gangsters?' said Callaghan. 'I wouldn't take much notice of what he says. Did he also tell you that I'm losing my marbles? That I'm going senile?

Making mistakes? Well, as your unfortunate experience last night might have suggested, nothing could be further from the truth.'

'Do we assume that the guns came in somewhere else then?' asked Blizzard.

'That's for you to find out,' said Callaghan. 'But you might as well know that I've been aware of Ray's little games right from the start. Many have underestimated me and come to pay the price. It's worth remembering that.'

He glanced at the wall clock.

'Anyway,' he said, 'I think that we have wasted enough time, don't you? Perhaps you would be so good as to close the door on your way out.'

'I think not,' said Blizzard.

The inspector glanced at Wendy Talbot, who walked up to the gangster.

'Nathaniel Callaghan,' she said, producing a set of handcuffs, 'I am arresting you on suspicion of bribing a police officer.'

Callaghan looked startled as Talbot produced a set of handcuffs.

'What the…?' he said.

'You do not have to say anything, but anything you do say may be used in evidence against you,' continued Talbot.

Callaghan stared at her for a moment, as if unable to believe what he was seeing. Before he could react, Talbot had twisted his arms behind his back and applied the handcuffs.

'You could get ten years for this,' said Blizzard. 'You'll be in your eighties by the time you come out.'

Callaghan glared at him.

'I knew you were the trouble the moment I met you,' he said. 'I should have sorted you out a long time ago.'

Talbot led her prisoner into the reception area where Blizzard pointed to the wall clock.

'See, Cynthia,' he said with a cheery smile, 'I told you that it would be less than ten minutes.'

The secretary glowered at him but did not say anything, instead watching in amazement as Talbot led her boss down the stairs, past his bodyguard and out to Blizzard's car.

# Epilogue

Eight months later, Blizzard and Colley were at Leeds Crown Court to see the final chapter in the investigation play out as Nathaniel Callaghan was sentenced after being found guilty of bribing Matt Riley, following a two-week trial. The previous week, the former detective had received a five-year sentence on his corruption charge, the judge having taken into account the way that he had co-operated with the CPS lawyers who were putting together the case against Callaghan. A month before that, Blizzard and Colley had been at the Crown Court in Hafton to see Ray Varone jailed for twelve years after admitting the conspiracy to murder charge in relation to the death of Alan Steele.

Now, Nathaniel Callaghan had been jailed as well and there had been judge's commendations for Blizzard, Colley and Talbot for their roles in the inquiry.

'Six years,' said Colley once he and Blizzard had escaped the attention of the media scrum outside the court and sought refuge in the busy city streets. The sergeant shook his head. 'It's nowhere near long enough, is it? I mean, he'll be out in three, won't he?'

'I'm not sure about that,' said Blizzard. 'If you ask me, it could be as good as a life sentence. You saw him in the dock, David. He's looking really old. Wendy reckons that the only way that he will come out of prison will be in a box.'

'He certainly didn't look well. Did I hear you say that she thinks he might be showing the signs of early-stage dementia?'

'That's what she said.'

'Life does have a gift for irony, doesn't it?' said the sergeant.

'Doesn't it just?' said Blizzard.

## List of characters

*Hafton Police Officers:*

DCI John Blizzard – head of Western Division CID
DI Graham Ross – head of forensics in Western Division
DS David Colley
DS Alan Steele
DC Jenny Carr
DC Sarah Allatt

*County force:*

Detective Superintendent Arthur Ronald – head of CID in the southern half of the force (which includes Western Division)
Marie Lindsay – press officer

*Other law enforcement officers:*

Retired Inspector Charles Radley – Hafton Police
Retired DCI Neil Sykes – South Yorkshire Police
Jane Kenworthy – MI5 officer

DS Matt Riley – West Yorkshire Organised Crime Unit (seconded to National Crime Agency)
DI James Rowles – West Yorkshire Organised Crime Unit
Wendy Talbot – National Crime Agency
Retired DS Michael Quigley – South Yorkshire Police

*Gangsters:*

Nathaniel Callaghan
Willy Jacobs
Edward Marston
Gary Race
Bobby Ross
Ray Varone

*Others:*

Cynthia – Nathaniel Callaghan's secretary
Gerald Crabtree – lawyer
Fee Ellis – Blizzard's girlfriend and mother of his son
Bob Harrold – cameraman
Sally Jackson – television producer
Edward Janes – drug dealer
Janice – Alan Steele's sister-in-law
Carl Latheran – drug dealer
Mikey – Blizzard's son
Peter Reynolds – Home Office pathologist
Jenny Morton – newspaper reporter
Claire Steele – Alan's wife
Charlie Walters – drug dealer

If you enjoyed this book, please let others know by leaving a quick review on Amazon. Also, if you spot anything untoward in the paperback, get in touch. We strive for the best quality and appreciate reader feedback.

editor@thebookfolks.com

www.thebookfolks.com

## ALSO BY JOHN DEAN

*In this series:*

The Long Dead (Book 1)
Strange Little Girl (Book 2)
The Railway Man (Book 3)
The Secrets Man (Book 4)
A Breach of Trust (Book 5)
Death List (Book 6)
A Flicker in the Night (Book 7)
The Latch Man (Book 8)
No Age to Die (Book 9)
The Vengeance Man (Book 10)

*In the DCI Jack Harris series:*

Dead Hill
The Vixen's Scream
To Die Alone
To Honour the Dead
Thou Shalt Kill
Error of Judgement
The Killing Line
Kill Shot
Last Man Alive
The Girl in the Meadow

*Writing as John Stanley:*

The Numbers Game
Sentinel

When a routine archaeological dig turns up bodies on the site of a WWII prisoner of war camp, it should be an open and shut case for detective John Blizzard. But forensics discover one of the deaths is more recent and the force have a murder investigation on their hands.

After a family is brutally murdered, one child is never found. It still troubles DCI John Blizzard to this day. But new clues emerge that will take him deep into the criminal underworld and into conflict with the powers that be. Cracking the case will take all of the detective's skills, and more. Coming out unscarred will be impossible.

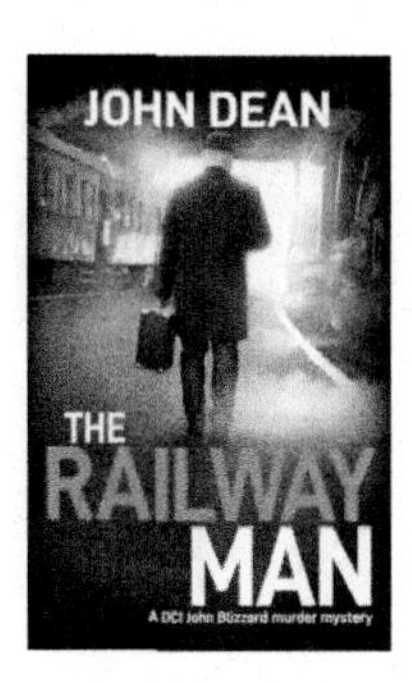


Veteran crime-solver DCI John Blizzard is confronted with his hardest case yet when a boxer and wide boy is found dead in a railway signal box. Someone is determined to ruin the investigation and prepared to draw the residents of a local housing estate into a war with the police to get their way. Has the detective finally met his match?

While detective John Blizzard looks into a series of drug-related deaths, his nemesis, gangland thug Morrie Raynor, is released from prison. Blizzard becomes convinced Raynor is linked to a new crime spree, but with little evidence other than the ravings of a sick, delirious man, the detective's colleagues suspect his personal feelings are clouding his judgement.

A corrupt industrialist is found dead in his home. When his family shed crocodile tears, DCI John Blizzard turns the screw. But when their alibis check out, can his team track down the real killer among a long list of likely suspects?

An undercover detective is shot in his home. Later, police officers on a routine patrol are fired at. Someone has a big problem with law enforcement. DCI Blizzard starts a crackdown on his city's most notorious gangsters. But is he in danger of rubbing the wrong people up the wrong way? Or is he already on the killer's list?

Someone is starting deadly fires, but the only clue to their identity is the obscure poetry that DCI John Blizzard receives on his desk. Taunting the police is one thing. Taunting Blizzard another. He'll stop at nothing to crack the case and collar the arsonist.

No-nonsense detective John Blizzard faces a difficult case when the matriarch of a criminal family is found dead. He must act quick to stop the situation from escalating into a gangland war.

When a dangerous convicted felon is released from prison, DCI Blizzard makes it clear he is unwelcome on his patch. But when a local church takes the man in, Blizzard has to deal with the community uproar. When a local youth is killed it will take all of the detective's skills to right a wrong.

When a youth is scared out of his wits in the local church graveyard by a man dressed all in black, the police don't think much of his tales about a bogeyman, but they are forced to take them more seriously when a murder later takes place there. DCI John Blizzard will have to suspend disbelief and work out the identity of The Vengeance Man before he wreaks havoc in the neighbourhood.

Printed in Great Britain
by Amazon

27630927R00118